W9-ASI-753

The Last Time I Saw You

Chicago Public Library
Avalon Branch
8148 S. Stony Island Ave.
Chicago, IL 60617

The Last Time I Saw You

by Rebecca Brown

City Lights Books
San Francisco

Copyright © 2006 by Rebecca Brown
All Rights Reserved

10 9 8 7 6 5 4 3 2 1

Cover design: Stefan Guttermuth
Text design and composition: Harvest Graphics
Editor: Robert Sharrard

A Cataloging-in-Publication record has been established for this book
by the Library of Congress.
    ISBN-10: 0-87286-447-2
    ISBN-13: 978-0-87286-447-4

www.citylights.com

CITY LIGHTS BOOKS are edited by Lawrence Ferlinghetti and
Nancy J. Peters and published at the City Lights Bookstore,
261 Columbus Avenue, San Francisco CA 94133.

R0409028889

Acknowledgments:

These pieces have previously appeared in the following magazines and anthologies in either the same or slightly different forms. The author is grateful to the editors who solicited and encouraged these pieces.

Ploughshares, ed. Amy Bloom

The Literary Review, ed. René Steinke

Zyzzyva, ed. Howard Junker

Chicago Review, ed. Andrew Rathman

Northwest Edge: Fictions of Mass Destruction, ed. Lydia Yuknovitch

14 Hills, ed. Jason Snyder

lowblueflame.com, ed. Brian Pera

Bookmarks/Seattle Research Institute, eds. Brian Goedde and Megan Purn

Bucknellonline magazine, ed. Carla Harryman

frisk, ed. Trisha Yost

Arcade, ed. Kelly Walker

Encyclopedia, vol. 1, A–E, eds. Tisa Bryant, Miranda F. Mellis, and Kate Schatz.

Contents

The Trenches

When we were kids we were a gang. There was only one other girl, somebody's little sister who we didn't like but her mother was never home so her brother had to bring her. We made her be the enemy or a spy or defector or someone already dead or being tortured though sometimes we let her be the nurse if she would go beg somebody's mother for something for us to eat and bring it back for us. Except for me, there was only her. I didn't want to be like her and I didn't want them to think of me like her. At first she tried to tag along with me but after a while she gave up. We all rode bikes together, the rest of us. She only had a trike. We played tree forts and baseball and football and soccer and war. We played in our yards and in the alleys behind our yards and in the vacant lot with all the broken bottles and piles of ancient dog shit and the brown flowered sprung out couch and down past where the road ended and there was a ravine.

We slid down the ravine and scraped our elbows and hands and tore the backs of our pants and coughed on the dirt we had stirred up and ripped our shirts. There was one boy a few grades ahead of us but the rest of us never thought it was strange that we were the ones he played with. I don't know if he thought about this, then or ever. I hope not. He didn't need to be more miserable than he was. Nobody should be that miserable. He was the one who had learned about "The Trenches" in school. He told us about them.

The Trenches, he said, were terrible, truly terrible.

The Trenches. The way he said it, the way we all said it forever afterwards, was never merely "trenches" with a little "t"; but always "The Trenches," capitalized. *The Trenches*. How we loved to say the words! *The Trenches! The Trenches! The Trenches!*

We went to the bottom of the ravine in the muddy creek bed where water sometimes ran until our shoes got wet and pretended that we had been, for months, in The Trenches. We pretended that our feet were white and peeling and soft as worms and that we had "Trench foot," "Trench mouth," "Trench fever." When we had to go home we crawled around in our front yards, beneath the box hedges that we pretended were trees in the Black Forest and under clothes lines that we called Electric Wires, and we screamed and grimaced as we climbed over the chain link fences between our yards as if they were electrocuting us. We spread dirt and grass and water from the garden hose on our faces to make us look like we had gotten muddy and sweaty from crawling in the jungle in the Philippines or were in camouflage. We flung ourselves on the ground and shouted, "I'm hit! I'm hit!!" then crawled along as if our legs were broken and our guts were hanging out, trying to get back to our buddies. Then we made more shooting sounds and flipped up off the ground and twisted around in the air then fell back down again and cried and moaned in cheerful agony "I'm hit! Oh God, Oh God, I'm hit!" Then we would groan crawl scrape ooze collapse until one of our brave buddies braved his way out across the bloody body-strewn battlefield to drag us back away from the machine gun fire torpedoes bombs bazookas machetes grenades Gatling guns missile rockets bottle rockets Molotov cocktails cannonballs hydrogen bombs and A-bombs.

The Trenches were terrible. Truly terrible. The Trenches were full of rats and mud and sewer water up to your ankles. The rats were huge, as big as cats, and always hungry, ravenous—they could eat a horse—with huge sharp dripping teeth and they carried horrible excruciating incurable diseases. The Trenches were always cold and dark and slimy and also had snakes in them, huge fat ones, as gross as eels, as strong as boa constrictors, and fast skinny ones more poisonous than the rattlers we had in Texas. The Trenches also stank from all the guys who hadn't taken a bath in months but also, even more in fact, they stank from all the terrible, horrible, grotesque wounds the guys had gotten that had been left untreated. The guys had arms—whole arms or parts of arms—shot off so they couldn't even hold their guns with both hands, just one, or a nub but they did hold their gun, if it was the last thing they did, by God, they held their gun. They had legs shot off, one or both, all the way or part of the way, below the knee or in the middle of the thigh so they couldn't walk any more, just hobble and lurch and fall around, knocking against the sides of The Trench or against each other. Sometimes they'd have to grab you to keep from falling and it was like being grabbed by a zombie. They dragged themselves along the ground through the mud and snakes and sewer water, their smashed crushed limp paralyzed lacerated legs or parts of legs dragging behind them like bags of sand.

They also had their guts shot or stabbed or bayonetted out, or not even all the way out, just part of the way out, which was worse, because you were still alive and could feel everything. Your guts and stomach and intestines were hanging out and you had to hold on to them to keep them from falling into the sewer water where the rats would eat them while they were still partly attached to you and you could feel the horrible rats' filthy diseasey teeth eating you.

We loved this. We loved being the men who lived in The Trenches doing what had to be done. Nobody else would do it but it had to be done so we did it.

Of course some of them died which is when you would have to lie there still until it was time to go home for dinner or he said you could be alive again for another assault. You didn't want to die early because then there was nothing to do. You just had to lie there and people could walk on your dead body and you couldn't do anything because you were dead.

In some ways, though, the ones who died were actually the lucky ones because the ones who didn't die suffered, they really, truly suffered. The suffering guys would beg to be put out of their misery. When you could you would. You would shoot them in the face, right between the eyes or put the barrel of the gun right on their temple and shoot them there. But that was only if you could. Because sometimes you were so low on ammo you couldn't afford to waste one single bullet on a guy of yours who was suffering, even if he was begging, pleading, really, truly suffering because you might need that very bullet, it might be your very last, to shoot some Jap or German or spy or whoever was coming into The Trench. So sometimes you had to bludgeon your guy with the butt of your gun or put your boot on his throat and press or just strangle him with your bare hands. Even then, that was only *if* you could! *If* you were lucky! And that's a big *If!*

If, for example, you were *not* being bombarded at that very moment by an entire platoon of rabid insane Japs or grenaded by a battalion of ruthless sadistic Germans in which case your guy just had to sit there and suffer, truly suffer, while you tried to hold off the entire Japanese battalion on your own. You couldn't take care of him while he was laying there suffering or if he was still mobile, and going insane, crawling around on what was left of his bloody stumps of legs and arms which were bloody as meat bones, bloody as T-bone steaks, bloody as dog food, bloody as the dog itself after it was hit by the Camaro, because you had to do what you had to do.

Actually, though, it was often the girl who was just laying there, so *she*, not *he*, had to just lay there. Hanging onto her stomach and guts and intestines as we instructed her or her head where her brains were oozing out or her ear was flapping off or her one eye—the other one was just an empty socket—which had been half shot out was hanging down.

We loved—we *loved*—to play like this.

We all said that some day we could do this all for real.

Actually, though, some of the horribly wounded guys in The Trench had been treated, but only superficially because we didn't have the right supplies. We could only wrap our bloody stumps with filthy, crusty, bloody, raggedy wrappings that had previously been wrapped around some other guy whose arm or leg or head had been blown off. Then after he had died we took the wrapping off and put it on another guy who was still living even if the new guy might get the dead guy's germs because it was better to only take the chance of getting your buddy's germs and dying rather than definitely dying because you lost all your blood, so we wrapped ourselves with filthy crusty rags that had the blood and brains and guts of other dead guys on them around our wounds, which, dangerous at it was, was also like Blood Brothers, even if it was being Blood Brothers with a dead guy, which was good to be.

No one wanted the girl's rags and she didn't try to make us take them but sometimes there was no alternative so we took them anyway and she didn't try to stop us. After a while, she stopped trying anything. She stopped doing anything.

On the other hand, we could also wrap, if there was anything left of them, our own ragged bloody sleeves or pants' legs or socks or whatever around our bloody stumps.

In The Trenches the guys could only "amputate"—we loved that word too—with their own knives or bayonets, which were steak knives or bread knives, blunt and bloody or serrated, as opposed to doctors' knives which would have been sterile and sharp, but we had to do it all without medicine or anything to put you under. Only, sometimes, if someone had saved some, you could have a swig or a slug of rum or whiskey. One time someone actually did bring a bottle from their father's house, Scotch Malt Whiskey, and we all tried it, even the girl. Her brother held her mouth open while the boy who was a few grades ahead of us poured it in, almost all of which I watched although at the very last I closed my eyes which I hoped no one noticed. But then right after that I very quickly drank my slug myself.

But mostly there was no medicine or whiskey so you had to bite on a bullet to keep from yelling out loud. Or if not a bullet, because you didn't even have any bullets left, not one single bullet left and now you were just sitting in the The Trench like sitting ducks waiting to get it, you would have to bite on the bloody rag of someone who died before you. Then you would taste their blood, which tasted like metal, and sometimes their brains which, he told us, tasted like chicken. You had to put something in your mouth because no matter how much pain you were in you couldn't scream or moan because the Japs might hear you and find you. You had to be absolutely completely silent. (The girl became the best at this.) If you made a sound your buddies had to hit you for your own good and for the good of the company. Sometimes we put a handkerchief in the girl's mouth even if she wasn't making noises. Her brother held her down and put it in and after a while she didn't even squirm.

When we had to come home from The Trenches at night, we did what we could get away with. We spread Mercurochrome all over our hands and legs and arms and called it "blood." We drew stitches on our arms and heads and legs and guts with magic markers. One time someone had a jar of mayonnaise and we blobbed it on like pus. We walked with limps we called our "war wounds," and lurched along like Frankenstein and flapped our arms around or dragged our knuckles along the ground like apes, as if our backs were broken and we couldn't stand up straight. Once we saw a man like that, or a kid, we couldn't actually tell. We couldn't tell how big or small or old he was or even if it was a guy or a girl. He couldn't stand up and his arms flapped around but we didn't think of him like a guy who got a war wound in The Trenches. We didn't think of things like that.

This is what we did when we were kids.

Then we grew up.

An Augury

You bring me breakfast in bed and have my tea leaves read before I am awake.

I didn't know this at first. At first I only heard the clatter of teacups, the muffle of your kicking closed the door. "Where are you going?" I cried, half asleep, and heard your muffled voice from down the hall: "Mmmm-mmmm-mmmmm!" It sounded like singing, singsong and sweet. It sounded cheerful. I liked that sound. I liked the sound of you around. But I had no idea what you said.

I tried to wake up earlier but I take time.

Your trench coat was tossed across the foot of the bed.

A week or so after you'd moved in—Did I mention the place had been only mine? That you'd moved into my apartment? I'd wanted you to, of course. I had invited you. Oh how I had invited you! I wanted you near me all the time and told you so. You always had admired the place and you had no place of your own.

I learned much later, too late I think, that you, in fact, had nothing.

I had coaxed and I had begged. I'd almost have done anything. I promised. You laughed with me, affectionately, I thought, and said "OK." That is, you said "MMMmmmmmmm," which I thought meant "OK" because we cast whoever's caution to the wind, or so I said, and you laughed at that, though you didn't ever really actually laugh, not out loud, more half a smile, a raise of half your mouth. Then you moved in with me.

It didn't take long because you didn't bring much. Besides, I had enough for both. I had a lot, I thought.

You used to live in a boarding house, a place down near the docks, where drifters lived, until you moved into my apartment. Or *our* apartment, rather. It took a while to get used to saying that. Our this. Our that. Our everything. You told me, anyway, to watch what I said. I tried.

After a while I woke up early enough in the morning to see you leave. I'd hear, or think I almost heard, the swish of the spoon in the cup of tea and then your mumbling voice, unruffled, calm, and saying things I couldn't hear, not words exactly, but something wise, more wise than words. But by the time I awoke enough to see, to lift mine eyes, oh lift mine eyes unto you, you were leaving. You had already left.

You always had already left.

And you always had coffee anyway, and it was always black.

One morning, though, when I awoke on time, we stood in the bathroom next to each other. We stood in front of the mirror and we were brushing our teeth and washing our faces and wiping the sleep away from our eyes, well, my eyes. You weren't. I don't know when you ever slept. In any event, we were standing together, though not together exactly, rather side by side. You were looking down into the sink. Perhaps you were spitting. I think this was the case because when you next looked up your teeth were clean. Your pretty white shiny lovely teeth were shiny and white and clean and there were these little bubbles of something at the corners of your mouth. I was looking forward, up, across from me, directly in the mirror where I saw the top of your head, your lovely head, the top of which (you'd taken your fedora off) was, to me, as if the sun, as if the pinnacle of heaven, all the milky sticky stars, the tip of the top of the universe, the boss of all that was. I was also looking at my face which was my usual face blah blah blah except for my—something? What?—My eyes. They looked blurry.

Then like they weren't quite there. Like they were being rubbed out. Like a job an eraser had not quite done. Like a Xerox of a painting that had faded in the sun or like a picture drawn with the stub of a colored pencil that was at its end. A picture drawn on wet paper smudging like fog as if like in steam coming up from vents. I almost couldn't see them.

"Does anything look weird to you?" I asked, still looking as much as I could into the mirror.

I think you looked. That is, I remember the feeling of movement but I was seeing less by the instant. Things were getting dark with only faded fields of black and gray and movement such as the movement of your head up to look at the mirror whereon our two faces, yours and mine, were or would have been reflected though I am guessing now, having by then completely lost all my ability to see—I could not see—and you said, "MMMMmmmmm?" Or perhaps asked, for it sounded like a question, the purr from your throat sliding up like a cat's, as if you were wondering, sort of, but also thinking of something else: "MMmmmm-mmm?" Or so I thought. For it was beginning to sound like steam in my ears like the hiss of the steam rising up from vents, like the slush of ice slushing back and forth on the windshield of a sedan.

I remember trying to grab with my hand. I must have dropped my toothbrush for I must have been brushing my teeth too for we did everything together then I thought because we liked to. Our this, our that, etc.

"Does something look weird to you," I asked, having stumbled, almost fallen in my sudden dark, having grabbed the edge of the sink, not you, for I was beginning to learn.

You didn't say anything.

Not even "MMMMMMmmmmm."

"My eyes looked blurry," I said, like the colors of them had faded, if there had in fact been color, not only black and white, which is, at last, how I remembered seeing, "then disappeared and I can't see you anymore."

I can't see anything anymore.

You took me to bed. Although I couldn't see, I knew it was you.

Besides I have never forgotten the touch of your hands, the way you held me and guided me, the way you knew and looked forward to, as you told me, once, I think, each thing and every single thing we did.

You knew before myself as if you made me.
You knew before it happened that it would.

You put me in the bed and then you fed me an invalid's food: a cup of tea. You took it upon yourself to care for me, a poor, poor invalid, a poor, poor widow without a mite. You are good to me! You gave me a room. You set it up as a sick-room and you kept me there. You let me stay, like a Samaritan, in your apartment.

I was grateful to you and tried to tell. My frustration is that what had happened to my eyes, as if some white thing had grown over them, as if some rubbery skin had sealed them, as if some wax, some plasticy rubbery melted thing had happened to my mouth as well because all I could say was "MMmmmmmm."

But I want you to know and I hope you do, that it means, that is, *I* mean: I owe you, Dear, for everything that I can never tell.

You knew what would happen before it did.
You also must know now, I assume, the only thing I know anymore is the truth.
I lay unmoving on the bed and imagine the sound of rain.

Other

There are no others. There only was the one.

Well of course there were others, but they were different, they didn't compare, they were a whole different league a whole different ball game.

The others came only later. After one could walk again and after the eyes no longer glazed, the hands no longer shook, the wrists no longer oozed but only dryly, whitely bore what one could claim were artfully, fashionably cut scarifications. One then experienced multitudes, made in fact a project of investigating closely, briefly, nocturnally, penetratingly both digitally and orally, first singularly, then in pairs, then severals (many of them were good about this: it has something to do with politics and property, about not owning or possessing. I never understood what they were nattering on about) then packs, slews of them.

Those poor miserable gals probably didn't know what hit them, them cracking open this little can of worms and the can spewing out all over them, us, one, that stuck to us, that sticks to one, that sticks the guts together, that cements the brain, that chokes one in the dreams. Those poor decent gals didn't know what hit them; they signed up for a diddle but got a baseball bat instead. They are, one must say, a sympathetic lot; they never, nary a one of them, called in the local authorities or had one arrested or hauled to the bin. They merely covered their faces with their arms and shooed or showed one to the door with instructions to never return, never show one's sick perverted brain-fucked face in their bed, town, hemisphere, whatever, again.

You never told me to get over you. You never told me to forget. I didn't. I remember you.

There were others, many good or kind, with better spirits. There were, indeed, rich handsome ones and gentle, wise, intelligent ones. There were compassionate ones and passionate. There were cute, delightful, darling ones. Among them even sexy ones.

Why didn't I attach myself to one or another or several of them?

Why did I only attach myself to you?

Why did I tape glue mucilage super glue my skin, my bloody flesh? Why did I nail my hands and feet? Why did I swing by a rope from the thought of you? Why did I pushpin, thumbtack, staple—both hand-held and power gunned—myself to you? Why did I tack and stick myself? Why did I drain my carcass, shellac my skin, cram myself into a pendant and hope you'd wear what I had been around your neck? Why did I, like a sucker a lamprey a limpet a barnacle an octopus, suck my greedy voracious though effective, one thing about which we both agreed, greedy greedy sucker to you and not let go? Why did I attach my mouth my tongue my teeth my fingers my wrists my arteries my sloppy throat my beating begging jugular the chambers of my poor misguided dumb and bloodied messy heart to you?

Because you had told me, limp and naked, barely capable of speech, the mouth having been previously, and very happily it seemed to me occupied, you loved me.

You said you were my twin, my self, my other. You said that I was who you might have been. You said there were no others. Well of course there were others, there wasn't something wrong with you, you were certainly desirable to others, but not like this, not like me. The others, you said, were trifles, slight, mere entertainments or obliged. They were different, they didn't compare, they were a whole different league, a whole different ball game.

You said this to me more than once. You said it to me knowing. You said it when the mouth the tongue the teeth the tongue were otherwise unoccupied, when, it seemed to me, for I was young, there was no reason to say anything unless it was the truth.

* * *

This was many years ago.

Now I can say with all the experience of the intervening years, the perspective, the wisdom I have gained having grown and learned and at much great, great length reconsidered that if one could, if I was given half a chance, I would not hesitate. I would. I would go back and do it all again.

I still believe it was worth it. Maybe "worth" isn't the right word. I still believe it was It? Not quite. Oh well. I still believe it was worth each time I threw myself against a brick or glass or electrically charged fence, each time I needed then drilled knocked blasted hacked or gouged another fucking hole in my fucking head. I still believe it was worth every time I tried to yank you back, every time I flung myself to where you were, each fete and do and soiree and affair and opening and invitation-only bash I crashed, flying in from the rafters, popping up from beneath the bed, leaking out of the heat vents, pushing up through the radiator pipes, splattering myself against the front end of your car like a deer in the headlights who waited for you, who sought you out when you drove home smashed again from yet another stupid idiotic party you'd performed at. I still believe it has been worth each time I've busted into your tidy little excuse for a life, each time you were screwing some poor well-meaning jerk and just when you really shouldn't have, thought of me, and that poor clueless sensitive jerk said, Hey, is something wrong? and you made up some trashy lie.

It has been worth each time you pretended you didn't know me when you ran into me in public, then how your stomach clutched and you excused yourself to the powder room and there puked up your guts into the toilet and/or splashed water on your face and though you hated to look at yourself made yourself, stared at your lying face in the mirror and wished you had the balls to blow out your brains. It was even worth those couple of B-release movie afternoons when I went to you, catching you when things weren't going so well at home, and you ushered me in quickly so no one would see me, then welcomed me with your outstretched arms, dropped your dress skirt blouse pants undies onto the fabulously parqueted floor and after we'd gotten the business over with, broke down confessed wept, said you were so sorry, oh, so so sorry and that now, yes, finally, now, yes, now you understood. That your whole fucking life (I paraphrase) was a complete and utter fucking sham and if only I would understand.

But I did understand. I do. I have for years. It isn't the understanding that's the problem. Needless to say, I said none of this to you.

You started making your stupid facile promises again, the ones you've never kept and never meant to, to meet me if only I'd give you a little time to tie some things up, etc. . . .

For God's sake, how do you live with yourself? You've got to be sick.

I've known for years what's sick about you. In fact, I confess, I may have even had an inkling of it very early on. However, it has only lately occurred to me what a major sicky yours truly too has to be to play along, to have played along with you for years. At least you've gotten on with your life, as paltry and as much of a crock of shit as it may be. Whereas I have stayed stuck in the past. Not entirely, of course. There have been others, as I believe I mentioned earlier, in the words of a garrulous and largely appetited former acquaintance.

There were others and I apologize for how I was with them. I am ashamed of all the times I spewed the debris of my ludicrous past on those well-meaning, decent people who tried to love me. I regret and I am sorry for the thoughtless things I know I must have done but do not remember because my memory is, at best, selective. Is, in fact—the better half thereof—a mess. I have these ridges, these ruts, these craters in my brain from where the glaciers move so slowly. I can't get out of them.

The past no longer happens and it cannot be undone.

I have been told to move along and get on with my life. Perhaps my life is to remember what is past.

The past is remembered differently. It can be different inside oneself and different also between two different ones.

Memory is its own kind of ill. It has its way of staying or returning. It can return in a spasm, a gasp. It can remain.

I'm sorry. I'm sorry for everything.

May God have mercy upon our souls.

Trying to Say

I am moving my mouth but nothing is coming out.

I am opening my jaws and my teeth are clacking and I am trying to push something up and out of my throat a lump a knot a ball a gag but either it's caught or it's permanent and can't come out, won't go back down, or at least not without tearing everything up like rusty wire like broken glass like rocks against my skin, like sandblasting my innards. I can hear my bones move deep inside my ears and my retarded—excuse me—developmentally disabled moronic stupid blithering tongue is flapping away like an idiot a ticker tape a flag on the Fourth of July the wagging foot of a slobbering dog whose flabby guts are being rubbed by some pathetic oaf, but nothing is coming out. Nothing is coming out that you could answer.

I am trying to tell you something but I can't.

★ ★ ★

It isn't—oh, it couldn't be, not after all these years—*I love you*?

Or, *Please come back*?

It can't be any more, *What happened?*
Can it?

★ ★ ★

Favorite terrible memories I go back to despite the fact that they can still really torture me:

The day at the train.

The day on the bridge.

The walk down the mountain.

The afternoon in your backyard.

The walk in your neighborhood

that night when we saw that yellow light and heard those people running and we went to the park too. It was such a lovely park near where you lived, very civilized, and the yellow lights came on, all misty and romantic, the air looked like magic, full of shimmery spots. The lights looked kind of orange actually, not yellow, rosy and moist, and there was a sweet scent, some kind of flower, you would know what it was, I wouldn't. Maybe you said so. But maybe you didn't know. Maybe I only imagine this when I think of how many things you knew that I didn't or that I thought you knew. Aw gee, I thought you were the greatest! Anyway, everything smelled green and nice and clean, like spring was in the air! (It was November, actually, but no matter. It felt like spring. As if it should have been spring. So actually maybe that sweet smell was clumps of filthy wet decaying leaves piled up in the gutters or caught in the drains or rotting windfall worm eaten apples.) In any event, the road really was slightly wet, shiny under the street lamps, and lovely! Extremely lovely! The air was soft and warm and moist with new things about to happen, new green and tender yellow shoots and darling little bunny rabbits and eggs and lambs and so on so when we went back to your house we went to the living room and sat on the floor (we had already had a few drinks, each) where we had to be quiet because your daughter was asleep upstairs and I put a hand on you then both hands then my mouth my tongue on your neck, your perfect neck, my tongue on your perfect neck, then your beautiful perfect hands then your mouth on me then we went upstairs to your room.

★ ★ ★

The night in your room.
The night that never seemed to get dark enough.
(Your skin always looked kind of blue.)
Then the light of the morning in your room.
Then the next night. The next night
And so on.

It had been years already
I had wanted this.
I told you this.
That did it.

How much of you did I make up from the start? How much did I not see you at all? How much of what I "remember" was only made up in my head?

It went on for a while but then too long for you but you didn't know or only partly knew that, certainly didn't know how to say that or actually even have much of a chance to say anything because I kept saying, insisting. Or even if you had, it might not have mattered much because I kept hearing things you had not said.

Though I do, I think, remember you saying to me, "Your relationships take place in your head." Then rather than think about what that meant, assumed that you found me fascinating.

At first, invited, I kept coming back and back to you, *literally,* as in showing up at your doorstep, meeting you overtly for and in polite social situations (your friends who didn't know who I was were nice to me) and then for our covert private assignations with which you were, as I, happy for a while.

But also *figuratively,* as in I returned both *like* a figure, a fragment, the outline or shape of something, a form, a person thought of or seen in a specified way, a likeness of a person or thing, an illustration, a shadow to you, in your memory, I think, though I can't be certain because I can't talk to you, as well as I also return *to* a figure of you in that which is left of my own private want gouged, love slammed, envy eaten addle of a brain.

I do this (these) figurative returning(s) again and again, as if I were beating my head against a wall. (*Nota bene*: the simile of the wall here is meant only to suggest an upright structure of wood, stone, etc. serving to enclose, divide, support or protect a room, and of one (me) beating one's (my) head against it. It is meant to be only a *figure* of the intractableness that beating one's head against a wall ongoingly suggests. It is not intended to suggest an image of a physical battering of person (you).)

(*Nota bene* also—and I want this on the record—I never beat you repeatedly.)

For example, one of the walls in your house. Such as a

wall in the living room with the half wall high bookcases, your various cloth and paperbound volumes of classics, with which you were very generous, and the occasional glossy photo travel book though you didn't travel much. I didn't understand that because I loved to run around, but now, perhaps because I am at last beginning to settle down, I may be starting to realize that you didn't want to leave and/or ruin your life.

But I'm getting away from myself. Where was I? The bookcases. Right. Not a page of dreck upon them. Knick-knacks, few and tasteful (silver cup, Etruscan-style statuette, Venetian-style glass paperweight, Georgian-style silver candlesticks) on top of the bookcases. The fireplace, the tidy desk, small but classy, though you would never have used that word, the beige lampshade that threw that lovely toasty beige warm honey colored fleshy light over everything including ourselves.

Or a wall in the kitchen downstairs, though there wouldn't be many places one could actually beat one's head, what with all the hanging pots and pans and cabinets and counters and fridge. In fact, I think the only exposed wall space was above/behind the breakfast table which was against the wall so one couldn't beat one's head against the wall unless one were leaning over the table to reach the wall, in which case one wouldn't be close enough to get a really rousing, bloody, nose, lip and/or eyeglass splitting wallop in. Though one could, I suppose, sit in one of the chairs at the head or the end of the table and beat one's head against the wall while sitting down, but then I doubt one would get any real oomph behind it. Though I also suppose, now that I spend all my time thinking about it—and that's the real is the problem, isn't it? all this stupid thinking—if one moved one of the chairs at the head or the foot of the table, one could stand next to the wall and beat one's head. But why go to all that trouble when there are plenty of other walls in other rooms?

Such as the walls in the guest room where I, as your "guest" "slept," the wall opposite the (single) bed for example, which had only one framed picture, I think of a some calm quiet peaceful Dutch landscape thingy that even I could not disturb. There was also an unobstructed head beating sized place by the window in the "guest" room I snuck to when I snuck from your room after we had done what we had to do and wanted to do and would do again and again as long as we could for the foreseeable future, or so I came to believe and/because you never indicated any reason I or you might think otherwise. I had to get back to the "guest" room, so I would be there in the morning when your daughter woke up so she wouldn't see me with you.

Or your room, the room to which we waited, all day the days and the weeks I was there, to go to after your daughter had, at last, gone to bed and, we hoped, to sleep so she wouldn't hear what we were doing. The room wherein we grabbed bit pawed pushed tugged held slid cried out collapsed and then, after a brief period of respite, went at it again.

Why don't I let myself get over this?

* * *

I tell myself because some things remind me.

For example, the other day I saw a woman who reminded me of you: the shape of her face, her narrow cheeks, the unspeakably exquisite beautiful slender line of her almost perfect (yours was, in fact, perfect) neck with that bump which on a guy would be obtrusive and clunky, his adam's apple, but on you was perfect and whereupon I put my mouth tongue, etc., the sleepiness of her eyes.

Though many things remind me of you.

Sometimes everything.

There is a tumor in my throat. A gag.

★ ★ ★

"Reminded" or not, I go back, if no longer in the real physical geographic world, then at least in a *figurative* world where, I am loath to confess I live a substantial portion of my life, to "you," or rather, as you seemed to know before I did, to that place in my head where my relationships took place. Wherein I pulled yourself.

Returning to what I remember includes the way you rasped, pulling air out of your throat when your teeth were clenched and you almost couldn't say what you needed, though what you "said" was not actually "speech," as much as some kind of noise. (I am trying to understand how to say what we can't and I can't.) Then how you wilted, limp, around my hands my mouth, my flapping idiot tongue and told me, once, Remember this.

Maybe I should have known back then that remembering is what we do to something over. But I was young.

(You weren't. What's your excuse?)

I wonder what you know now but I don't know because I haven't been able to talk to you for years.

Though if I could, what would I tell you?

If I could, would I even want to?

Because if I can't, then I can remember (invent) whatever I want.

What might I try to say? *I have not forgotten you.* Duh. That doesn't even begin to describe it. I mean, I also "have not forgotten" loads of people: my high school gym teacher, Miss O'Brien, Casey and Crawford, the two boys down the street in Kingsville, my sister's first boyfriend who she said looked like Stephen Boyd and was a Jew which was a big deal in Texas then, Mary Kay Ellington, Mary Kaye Ethridge, Lydia and Kenneth, Sharon Whitely, who drove a stick shift station wagon, the girl we called Baby Face whose real name I actually can't remember, my brother's first wife, whose name I do remember but whose privacy I will respect, my father's second wife (ditto), my seventh grade Texas History teacher, Mrs. Duvall, the son of my seventh grade Texas History teacher, Evan Duvall, Bob Ewald, the chubby guy in 9th grade speech and drama who did the great Paul Lynde impersonation, etc., etc. I "have not forgotten" any of them either. "Not forgetting" doesn't even begin to get close.

Or, *I am still in love with you?* Closer, but still not right. I mean, honestly, even I can no longer call whatever this thing was/is ("Love seeketh not its something to blah blah . . ." "Love's not true love that something's blah blah blah . . .") love.

How about, *I am still obsessed with you?* Better. At least that doesn't dress it up as something nice. But I have to admit it isn't constant, it's only sometimes, only when I work on it, which also brings me to the fact that obsession, to me, at least in how I read the Webster's New World Dictionary, suggests involuntariness:

ob.sess (eb ses, ab—) **vt.** [< *L obsessus,* pp. of *obsidere,* to besiege , *ob (* see OB-) + *sedere,* to sit] 1: to haunt or trouble in mind, esp. to an abnormal degree; preoccupy greatly. (Second Concise Edition, 1975). (Which is also, in a fascinating, though only to me, coincidence, the year I fell in love with you! Or should I say, began about you to "obsess.")

It may have been the case back then that I/my mind was "besieged" "haunted" or "troubled" by something outside of itself, that I was acted upon, if not by you, by something else I couldn't control such as my body hormones mouth or brain. Who knows.

However, my being besieged is no longer the case. I am no longer an innocent youthful possessable passive vessel. I volunteer. I willfully purposefully doggedly (hey! there's a little in-joke there for any old reader friend who may still be with me, and if you are, I thank you) pursue follow chase desire this abnormally preoccupying mental trouble.

It is no longer, if it ever was, done unto me.

Now I do it.

Herein's a shame.

There are moments when some relatively benign thought of you wafts casually across some outskirt of my brain but rather than merely glance nostalgically toward or "recollect in tranquility" then wisely turn and let it go, or hoary headed, stoop shoulderedly with all the well earned wisdom of my age sigh "I shall be (trying to) tell(ing) this with a sigh. . . ," I instead, after an heroic labor of picking scratching worrying

digging around the scab of it, unstaunch unleash launch forth
what I've been itching to get back to, the one sharp thrust like
the poke of a poker up a hole, thereafter which I, gouged,
twist writhe struggle but do not let go. No, rather I invite the
jackhammer Gatling gun tongue swallowing spit flailing furniture breaking seizure that crashes hurtles spews busts over
into me. I give way to welcome chase indulge in actively pursue these thoughts, memories, internal electrical events, insis-
tently regretting, reliving, whatevering, wanting you. Then I
both consecutively and simultaneously hate that I do this and
that I do it willfully, despite (because of?) (and here's the real
shame) the fact that I now have a stable, good, decent, solvent,
healthy, well rounded, satisfying—and I really mean all that, I
am not being ironic—life.

Why do I do this?

I worry, whenever I get in this state, which I am embarrassed to admit is not as rare as one would hope, that I am not
merely going to turn back into my regular old nut case self,
but that I am currently, by virtue of having thoughts like
these within this otherwise decent life I lead, a complete
fucking sham.

Why why why why why, I repeat, do I do this?

The obligation of a promise?
A perceived promise? Whose?
A promise to remember? What?

Maybe it's because I've been forbidden to talk to see hear
from you. Maybe if you and I were in good old boring once
yearly when we feel magnanimous Christmas (or some other

more spiritually culturally or politically appropriate holiday) card and family photograph touch, I'd be able to roll my eyes and huff, in the snottily superior way I do about the others, "God, she's really going to seed," or "Same old plastic smile! When is she going to realize she is no longer the hot young thing?!" or "Jesus Christ, look at what a hairy old slob that husband is!!" or "Holy Mother of God, those kids look monstrous," or "Where on earth did she find that pathetic creature?!?!" or "What on earth did I ever see in her?" However, having forgone even this piddling contact—

I wonder if you decided to cut off all contact because however mistaken you may have been about you and me, you were at least able to retain or revive enough sense to figure out that if you and I kept in touch you and I would continue to have the same disastrous effects not only upon one another but also upon (talk about innocent bystanders!) everyone around us.

I often have to remind myself that much as I have tried to cast you as a coward, it's not like I put up any great protest. If I had protested or done some kind of carry-you-off-on-horseback thing, then I would have had to become responsible to you and your life and everything else that went with it and I sure didn't want to be saddled with that.

In retrospect, I see you made it easy for me.

In retrospect, I see that what you did was brave.

Or, I wonder, if we had been able to keep in touch, would we have turned into the same old ho hum, ex-whatevers the rest of them do? Like, if we'd stayed in touch, would we be actually slightly embarrassed that we had actually been whatever we had been?

Instead of being, as we are now fixated/obsessed/rendered senseless by it.

I say "we" but of course I have no idea about you. Maybe you haven't thought of me in years. Or thought of me only in the way that one would think of a funny old friend or one's junior high school Texas history teacher's son or Casey and Kenneth or Mary Kaye Whitely or whatever her name was.

Maybe you haven't because you got over whatever it was and now your life has became decent and good. I hope, I do actually really hope this is true for you.

Maybe I am, at last, beginning to think I might get over it too.

Maybe I am going back to this stuff now in the lurid, self-lacerating detail I am because I am able to now because my life has—and god knows how, I sure didn't make it happen—become truly good and decent and blessed. Because these days I am beginning to think that I am, not only loved but actually capable of giving love in return. Am beginning to finally feel not afraid of what this means. And maybe because now, at last, I am beginning to believe that I will not lose my marbles again, I can allow myself to slog back through the debris of my past in the hope that I might be able to understand it, and even—and this was inconceivable until recently—forgive it. Forgive you and all the other poor unsuspecting souls with whom I thereafter tangled as well as my equally poor pathetic unsuspecting self for what we did to one another.

31

Maybe if I can remember what really was I can begin to forget.

Maybe I can do this now because I am beginning to think I will not do it again.

Maybe I am trying to say *Forgive me.*

The Movie

I see this girl, this woman, hurrying down the hall. Tall, quick, competent, thin. Mid-thirties and extremely WASPy like she's in "the horsey set" or went to Smith or Barnard or somewhere. Sharp features, good bone structure, honey reddish hair. She reeks of money, of "breeding," like all the women who rode horses we saw when we worked at the country club, though they never had to say, rode "horses," they just said "rode" and everyone knew what they meant. I mean, as if they'd ever set foot, ass that is, on a bike. A *motor*-bike. And who played tennis and swam and rode around in their yachts which I only heard about because there wasn't a yacht place at this particular country club where we used to work. I was totally fascinated with them. I also really hated them. I also of course sort of wanted to fuck their brains out. And not nicely fuck their brains out but like really ripping their fucking Brooks Brothers or Saks Fifth Avenue or Neiman Marcus shirts, excuse me *blouses*, off so the buttons go flying across the room and bounce off the incredibly obscenely expensive Persian carpet their husband Perry or

Robert or Jonathan or whoever had had sent back from his most recent trip to the Middle East where he was dealing in oil or arms or something totally immoral and disgusting, yanking her bra off so hard the little bent metal thingies in the back twist open by themselves and I can hear it, the bra, bounce on the carpet too when I fling it down there and then Amanda or Elizabeth or Buffy or whoever, though we were never to call them that, not being permitted to address the members unless they addressed us first and then we were supposed to respond with Miss or Mrs. Whatever, DuPont or Hennessy or Hennessy-Fucking-Smith and me get down to business but of course I never did. Fuck their brains out or their asses into next year and leave them splayed there opened up like a fucking—whatever—

I have mostly tried to stop thinking about that kind of shit when I can.

So this totally WASP woman I see bustling down the hall is carrying a briefcase. The briefcase, needless to say, is fabulous too. Probably worth more than what I made in a month of working there. Two months. The WASP is thin, but she's also fit, athletic, and there's a way she moves, the length of her stride, the way her arms swing out in front of her, that I know for absolute certain she's a dyke and I'm saying this to someone sitting next to me—I don't know who this is, but it's someone I know—I say, "God, whatta dyke!" And my friend, because now I realize this person next to me is a friend, kind of snickers and says, "Yeah. But not my type."

Mine either. Not that she's bad looking. She's great looking in a rangy, preppy kind of way if you like that kind of thing. But it's her hair. It's too long. I have never gone with a

woman with hair that long. And that business suit drag—
navy skirt and blazer and pastel shirt—does absolutely nothing for me. As in Zero. Those types are so repressed. Anyway,
she's bustling down this gray awful looking hallway. It doesn't
actually have moisture seeping down it, but it's got that kind
of seedy atmosphere. Which might make you wonder what
she, Miss Perfect, is doing here in the first place, except that
it's clear she is on a Mission. Like Mother Fucking Teresa at
The Soup Kitchen or the Mayor's Wife at the The Homeless
Shelter. In fact, she looks completely Junior League-y.
AbsoLUTEly not my type.

Then I'm hearing this clanging noise and then there's a
burly guy in a uniform, like a cop uniform, which makes me
realize the clanging noise is a jail or prison cell opening or
closing. The guy nods at her and she nods at him like they
know each other because she's so fucking important. Now
the angle shifts and I'm seeing her from behind, (nice ass)
and, yup, she's heading towards an open prison gate. Now I
can hear her heels clicking. Not high heels because there is
nothing, absolutely nothing whorey about her, unfortunately.
She is so completely Junior League. I bet her shoes cost what
I—what we—both of us, would have made in a fucking
month of bussing country club tables. Two months. As she
gets closer to the gate two other burly uniformed guys—one
white, one black because even this slammer is so fucking
PC—nod to her and go through the gates with her.

Wherever she's going she ain't going alone, I think to
myself, and Jilly—because now I realize it's my old pal Jilly
sitting next to me in the dark, whom I haven't seen in ages—
snickers, "Too bad for you," as if she has read my thoughts

about this rich WASP girl not going to be alone. I punch Jilly's thigh and snicker like "we know what that bitch wants." I don't understand how Jilly can read my mind, but I love it.

Now WASPGirl and her burly guy-guy escorts are going through another set of prison bars, then another. I mean, honestly, how thick do they have to lay it on? We get that this place is dangerous but that WASPGirl is oh so very brave blah blah blah. But also, nothing ever happens to girls like that.

Jilly wants some popcorn but she wants me to get it.

"Get it yourself," I whisper, mock angry like we always used to. I can't quite see her silhouette next to me. From the light in front of us.

"Aw, come on . . ." Then, like she always used to say, "Just this *once*?"

I start to give my standard response but she's still going on. "One little tiny bag of popcorn? Pleeeeeeese?"

"Fuck you," I mutter affectionately. "Get it yourself," and I turn my legs to the side as if to give her room to get around me so she can go to the lobby and get the popcorn.

"Hey," she whispers, suddenly earnest, "I can't do that shit anymore. You know, like walk . . ."

"Wha—" I start to ask, but I don't want to get into all that. "OK, OK," I say, still mock angry. "Still with, right?"

"Yeah," she sighs. "Man, do I miss butter."

"Oh," I say. I don't know what else to say. "You want a Coke or anything?"

"Yeah. But . . . uh . . . nothing with caffeine."

Jesus. She used to be practically addicted to caffeine. Coffee, tea ("no herbal shit") Coke, Pepsi, Mountain Dew.

She actually enjoyed eating espresso beans. In fact, she could eat them *after* doing a double espresso after dinner and be none the worse for the wear. As soon as she hit the sack she could fall straight to sleep and sleep the whole night through like a fucking baby. Her favorite was Cherry Coke. She drank it All Day Long.

"You're not doing some weird diet shit are you," I say.

"Fuck no," she laughs. "Just no caffeine. I can't sleep . . ."

I don't want to ask.

"But everything else, pal, bring it on."

"Thank god," I laugh and I get up and go to the lobby.

I'm not the only one out there. There's a guy by himself. He looks out of place here, a little, well, classy actually. Silvery hair. Good shoes. Tweedy.

He isn't getting something at the concession stand. He's sitting at the window counter reading a newspaper. He glances up at me over his horn rimmed glasses. I look away. It's like he's hovering, like he's waiting for some girl or woman to flip out and have to leave and leave her boyfriend there to finish watching it alone and then he is going to follow her home.

"Two Cokes and a buttered popcorn," I say to the pimply kid behind the counter. He looks about fifteen and I'm suddenly thinking how awful it is, I mean, how truly awful it is if he has seen the movie now playing in the theater. Then I'm thinking he must have. I mean, what's he gonna do, take this shit job for minimum wage and *not* see every movie he fucking can? But Jesus Christ he's just a kid. Impressionable. He shouldn't be able to see this kind of shit. No wonder this country is so fucked up. I hate that.

"LargeJumboorGrande," he says.

"Uh . . ." I start and he points to the cups—one, two, three in order—sitting on top of the popcorn warmer. (Needless to say they don't pop it fresh here, they only spray the place with popcorn perfume and keep it under a heat lamp.) When he sees me look up at the 'menu' on the wall behind him he taps the cups again in order, and says, "One-seventy five, two bucks, two-fifty." Then he taps them a third time, "Twelve, twenty, thirty ounces."

I look at the cups. OK: Two times twelve is twenty-four. So the Grande thirty ounce more than twice as big as the Large but only seventy-five cents more. But then I think I shouldn't be cheap. I mean, when was the last time I saw Jilly?

Actually, I can tell you exactly when the last time I saw Jilly was and I don't care to think about that, thank you very much.

But then I figure it's my dime.

"Can you put two straws in the thirty ounce?"

"Yep."

It's not like I have any communicable diseases. Or even if that would matter. And as for me, if Jilly's got some weird thing now that would fuck me up, I say, hey pal, do me a fucking favor and bring it on. Jilly was always really healthy though. As soon as she moved into the empty room after FuckFace moved out, she taught me how to cook vegetables and made me them. Made me not buy only crap to eat. Hardly ever drank. Was always the one who saw we got home OK.

Jilly was always the one who was always careful.

Fuck.

"OK. A Grande Cherry Coke. Wait. Does that come in decaffeinated?"

"Nope. Only Coke."

"Oh . . . OK. Then a Grande Decaf Coke and a—"

The kid is about to start in on the LargeJumboorGrande version of the popcorn sizes but I stop him.

"The biggest popcorn you have. And lots of butter."

"It's not butter. Only butter flavoring."

"Whatever," I say. "Tons of it," and he scoops up a scoop of long ago popped popcorn into a huge waxy bag and squirts a few squirts of some yellowy greasy stuff on it.

"That enough?" he asks.

"A few more," I tell him and he squirts on more of the stuff. I douse the bag with salt, grab a handful of napkins and head back into the theater.

It looks like there's nobody else in there besides Jilly and me. Weird.

Now WASPGirl is sitting in a big gray room with one window up high in the wall with bars on it. The walls and the floor look concrete. Comfy, I think, with that snotty tone of voice I always used to use.

Then Jilly, again as if she's heard what I'm thinking, ribs me, "Needs a woman's touch. Curtains? I think I know just the little lady to do it!"

Maybe Jilly's taste has changed. Maybe the "little lady" on the screen has gotten to be her type. Which is actually pretty hard for me to imagine, but what do I know anymore? I rib Jilly back, but just as she's digging in to get a big handful of popcorn. I put the bag on the armrest between us.

"It's decaf," I whisper as I pass her the Coke.

She nods thanks and takes a big slurp. "Man, this is great," she says. "This is INCREDIBLE!"

What's the big deal, I'm thinking. It's a fucking Coke.

She hands it back to me and I take a sip. Tastes normal to me. I look at her like, "Wha—"

And she says, "It's been a while."

Then she turns back to the screen and for a second I watch the light flicker on her face.

I hadn't thought of that.

She grabs some more popcorn. I hear her hand scrabbling in the bag and then shoving a bunch in her mouth. I hear her chewing it, swallowing, her slight groan of pleasure. I hear it going down her throat. She grabs another handful. "This is tremendous, man," she says, "I *love* this."

Whatever.

WASPGirl is sitting across the table—a big painted metal or wood table, something impressive, across from this guy. You'd expect him to be seedy but he's not. He's actually kind of classy looking. Silvery hair, good bone structure. Like he could be a professor or a CEO or shrink. Except for his prison uniform.

Actually, wait a minute.

Now WASPGirl isn't sitting across a table from him, she's sitting at one of those prison talk things, where the guy sits on one side of a totally closed off partition and you sit on the other side so there's no way you can pass each other anything and so the guy can't grab your throat.

I turn to look at Jilly to see if she's registered this error in continuity. But she's not reacting. It's like everything's normal to her. Like she knows what's going to happen.

I do not know how she can fucking stand it.

"Jilly," I whisper. But she shushes me. Not jokey, though

like we always did, but tenderly. She puts her hand on my forearm very tenderly.

Now WASPGirl is sitting at one of those glass wall window things that separates prisoners from not-prisoners. The guy she is visiting is a very very very bad guy. The burly cop guys are in the room too, discreetly far enough away but close enough so that if the guy were to try anything the cop guys would be on him in a flash.

So why the fuck are they never there when you really need them?

There's a long, lingering, close up of WASPGirl's profile, her mouth moving, her lips opening and her tongue moving around, her lips coming together, pulling apart, coming together again, really slow and repeated. You can see little tiny points of saliva. Shiny pink lips. Wet mouth. It's really sexy. She is, in fact, talking, but somehow now the sound is gone so no one can hear. You're just looking at her wet pink soft red wet pink mouth move really close up and over and over again with no words.

I hate when they do this. Like girls' mouths aren't for talking, just for cock sucking. They want you to think that. I hate that.

I look over at Jilly and she is not smiling. She is not eating popcorn or drinking a coke.

The guy on the other side of the prison window thing looks familiar.

Jilly is just sitting there. Light is flickering on her face but somehow I can't actually see her face.

Now the this guy is wearing this totally disgusting dark

brown leather mask like a catcher's mask and dog muzzle combined. Like some medieval torture thing. It freaks me out to see it. To think about someone wearing it. To think about someone even coming up with the idea of it.

You can see this guy's eyes—blue gray, intelligent—because there are holes for his eyes in the mask, and you can see his mouth too because there is a hole there too, but the mouth hole has like these little bars in it, metal bars like in a prison because this guy's mouth, especially, as well as the rest of him, is *in prison*. And he is talking too. And though I can't hear the words he says, I can hear the tone of his voice. He sounds so calm. He really could be a professor or a shrink, someone rich and smart and better than you and compared to whom you do not even deserve to fucking live.

WASPGirl, however, who is elegant, pretty, classy, rich, smart, well-dressed and, clearly has "breeding" and so many other things I hate so much not only because they intimidate the fuck out of me but also because I just hate them, does deserve to live. In WASPGirl, in fact, MaskMan may have met his match.

Now the two of them are talking together. Now I can see both of their mouths move in sexy creepy close up. Now I can hear her voice too, not what she says, but the tone of it. It's modulated, intelligent, calm, just like his. They are sparring, having met their matches. Which is a really scary thought, but at least they have each other. They deserve each other.

Actually, though, I can't really go that far. As much as she drives me crazy, as much as I envy and hate her, I can't say anyone deserves him. I can't wish him on anyone. No one deserves that.

Still, if it *had* to be someone, I'd rather it be her than someone else.

He's talking to her through his muzzle mask, being charming and witty and erudite. I hate people like that. I wish they'd just lock them all up together and let them talk each other to death.

But she's rising to the occasion. Matching every smart literary and cultural reference of his with one of hers. And her grasp of logic, particularly forensic logic, obviously, is impeccable. Really quite impeccable. She is a very impressive girl.

OK. OK. What happens next? Does she try to enlist his help in some insidious project? Does he agree but then only to try to fuck with her brain even more? Because there's no one else she can go to to ask for help in this most recent whatever because there is no one up to the brains and imagination and inspiration that he and she have. Or maybe she's a brilliant shrink studying him for her new book about abnormal psychology. Or a brilliant lawyer trying to understand him so she can get a handle on a current string of copycat crimes. Or maybe her brilliant father was a serious nut case who was locked away forever for similar misdeeds, until the other guys in the slammer rammed the detached leg of the frame of somebody's prison issue and heretofore previously considered indestructible metal bed up his ass in their own form of "criminal justice" and she's always had this sick desire to learn what made her dead sick brilliant father tick. Or maybe a condition of MaskMan's sentencing is that he gets one visitor and, having read all of her brilliant legal treatises and blah blah blah or because she was the lawyer who sent him away for life and he knows her single passion, outside of law, is chess, he chooses her

43

and maybe they play chess once a month in person and the rest of the time in the mail. Or maybe —

Hell I don't know. And frankly, I don't want to know. And furthermore, I think it's appalling and sick that so many people *do* want to know. I mean, how fucking sick in the head can people get?

WASPGirl leaves the prison and goes home. She lives alone in a secure building. She has nice things. (Nothing too frilly or girlie; she is, remember, a dyke, though no one besides me and Jilly seem to get this. How can everyone be so blind? And why the fuck won't WASPGirl come out anyway? I almost do wish MaskMan would let her have it. Though I should never wish a thing like that on anyone because no one deserves that. No one.

Of course a lot of people don't deserve what they get, but they get it anyway and what the fuck can you do? Nothing. Fucking nothing.)

Jilly isn't eating popcorn any more. She isn't drinking decaf Coke any more. She looks like she is looking straight ahead except her eyes are closed.

I don't know what do to.

"Jilly?" I say. "Jilly? Jilly?"

It's the only sound in the room. It's like the sound when you wake up from talking in your sleep and you are alone.

"Jilly?" I say. "Do you want to tell me? What happened." She hesitates a moment then shakes her head.

I put my hand on her forearm. I try to do it like she did, tenderly. There's no more popcorn and no more Coke and she turns to look at me. She turns to me and I can see she has been crying. Her eyes are puffy and then I can see her face is scratched. Then it's like it's coming into focus, and I can see her face is bruised. Her hair is torn and her skin is torn. Then I can see black crusty stuff, her blood, all over her face and neck. She can't tell me anything because her lips are torn apart. One of her ears is dangling, chewed part way, and I want to look away but I don't because I think she wants someone to see. She wants me to stay with her a while. She doesn't want to be alone a while.

Then it's like I can see her whole self—no, that's not the word I want to use—like I can see her whole *body*—except it is no longer whole. It's all apart.

I try to not think of this happening. But she wants somebody to know.

So I look. Down at her torso and her limbs. What used to be her stomach and ribs and breast. I don't know what I'm looking at exactly but I keep looking. It's all a mess. Dark stuff and broken stuff, red stuff and yellow stuff. Stuff that looks like it used to be white. Soft stuff and torn apart stuff. Stuff that used to be her body.

I look a long time until I feel her looking at me so then I lift my eyes to look at hers. I can't really see her eyes but I don't look away.

The place that used to be an eye is closed and the white of it is red. What used to be a clear blue eye is black, as black as the eye of a dead black fish but she is looking into me so I don't look away.

She starts to open her mouth. Blood is coming up out of her throat and dripping down and I can see how hard it is for her to hold her head upright because her neck's broken. Her teeth are broken. Some of them are completely gone. The rest of them are pink and red and clotted and black. It hurts her now to try to talk.

I want to tell her she doesn't have to because I know what she's trying to tell me but I don't.

Is it "Be careful?" Or "Goodbye?" Is it ""Watch out—" Or "Don't—" Is it "Remember me?"

Then she is lifting her hand toward my face. She touches my face so tenderly. I reach up to put my hand on hers. It's cold. The flesh is wet. I want to pull my hand away but don't. I press my hand to hers as if I was holding it, as if I could hold it back together. I can feel all the little busted bones of her beneath the skin. I keep my hand on hers a while until I feel, beneath the broken bone and flesh, beneath the things he did to her, a warm thing that remains.

I try and try to feel this.

I turn back to the movie screen as if it could turn the sound back on and we could hear, could talk to each other again but everything's dark.

Then suddenly the air is cold and I'm feeling nothing in my hand.

I turn to look at her but Jilly's gone.

Pulled Up

You ask me where I am. I'm here. But part of me is somewhere else. I'm lying here with you, I'm looking at you, deeply in your eyes as if I see, as if I could and I am listening, trying hard, but part of me is being pulled away.

There is a hook that comes down from the ceiling and it goes between a pair of ribs and hooks beneath my sternum and yanks. There is something like a shot of light. I gasp. It feels very cold then hot.

"Are you OK?"

"Yeah . . . uh . . . a little chilled," I say. Surprisingly, there's hardly any blood. Not so's you'd notice. You swing your warming arm across me.

The hook is at the end of a rope or maybe a chain. I haven't seen this clearly yet, but whatever it is comes down from above me, that is, us. I'm sorry for that. This is not about you. I didn't want you to be part of this.

But it's happening to me again and it will happen over and over again. Even after I think it's done then it undoes itself and then does itself again.

Merely having something done doesn't get it over with.

I can't explain and wouldn't want to if I could.

The rope or chain is hanging from the white ceiling. I don't know if it's always there or just when I'm aware of it or just when it decides. I don't know why things are the way they are.

Do I only imagine the little flakes of white paint or insulation or drywall or whatever flaking, sinking, falling down, slow billowing like dandelion seeds or feathers or snow, cool on my face, my eyebrows? All clean, pristine and wintry fresh! As if things aren't the way they are. As if things might be different.

Whatever the white stuff is—I suppose it could be asbestos. God. I hadn't thought of that—falls on the back of your head but you are not aware of this. For which I'm grateful.

The hook just misses your pretty upper arm, your smooth, brown shoulder which you have kindly laid across my chest as if protecting me as if to hold. The smell of your skin is good like milk.

I'm hooked like a meat hook. Yanked.

I try to resist but it's hard.

"Are you sure you're OK?"

"Yeah. I'm . . . uh . . . I'm just rearranging myself."

You pull the blanket over both of us and curl over on your side. In no time at all you're breathing deeply, sleeping.

The rope or chain—why can't I see it clearly?—swings slowly back and forth either like someone was pushing or pulling it recently or even a long time ago in the past, but not for a while so now it is slowly slowing down or like something knocked against it a while ago or maybe it just goes on forever and ever like that pendulum at the Smithsonian. Christ, I don't know.

Oh, come on. If not me, who does know? This is not exactly a major studio release.

OK. OK . . .

So. Now it's slowing down a bit—it being the hook, which is a hook, not it the rope or chain or whatever—and appears to be dropping very, very slowly. I see it above the top of your shoulders, the back of your head. It's close, but it will not hook you. The most you might feel is a slight breeze from movement of the hook or rope or chain. The rope or chain appears to get longer as if it is being uncoiled from a coil above the hole in the ceiling. There must be a hole. Where the flakes of paint or plaster or snow or asbestos came from, from making the hole or putting the hook through the hole or from the movement of the rope or chain against the sides of the hole.

The chain is on a wheel above the ceiling. Then, what's past that? Another room? An open sky? My blue heaven? Who is uncurling it? Who lets it go?

It is not shiny or cheap or ridiculous like the pendulum in *The Pit and The Pendulum* with Vincent Price. Talk about hokey! Even when I was a kid I knew it wouldn't be like that. So cartoony. And that laugh of Price's? Spare me! But I actually really liked him a lot in *Atomic Cafe* when he played that crusty old guy who was trying to date again. Hysterical. I had to hand it to him. Also, Tom Jones in *Mars Attacks*. I love it when these old guys play parodies of themselves. It's the only way to go out—howling. I even went out and bought a Tom Jones CD, *The Lead and How to Swing it* which actually has some tremendous songs on it like:

If I only knew
what I could do,
to make you, make you love me.
(to make you, make you love me!)

There are a couple more good songs on it, but I can't remember how they start.

Where was I?

This hook is neither sharp shiny or hokey like in the Vincent Price movie but dull, workmanlike, a "working" as opposed to a "Hollywood" hook. It's also really, really big. Like if it fell on a concrete floor it would break the floor. Like it would break a boulder.

I try not to watch but I can't help but sense the movement swinging closer.

Now it's right above me. The hook is metal stainless steel with reddish brown bronzy colored dots, like lichen, but very smooth because it has been around a while. The chain is metal, with oiled squarish green gray silver black ovalish links. I can smell the oil. Clean like my grandpa's tool room used to be. He was a great guy. Dead now. The chain is a stainless steel twisted wire, an all natural fiber hemp rope as thick as someone's arm. The hook is not a fishhook like for fly fishing or trout but for something huge, a sturgeon, halibut, one of those big flat fat ancient flounders.

The hook could hold the carcass of a cow.

It swishes teasingly against my skin then drops sinks

pushes hard. There is a rip, a spurt, a dig. Down between my bones into the meat.

I say this is not about you but in some way of course it has to be because after all you are here. Though even as it digs inside my innards it remains above you, and you don't see it, I am afraid that it will not remain contentedly like this.

I can't believe it wouldn't get you if I stayed.

I'm sorry I didn't explain to you why I left. I'm sorry I left the way I did but I was afraid and that is the only smart thing that I have ever been.

A Ventriloquist

I live with a ventriloquist.

You think you hear me talking but it is not me. My lips and throat and tongue make noise but you don't hear me. No one does. It isn't me, it's who I live with. I am but her voice, her vessel. Less.

I once thought it was clever, like a trick that I enjoyed. I liked to laugh at others because they didn't know. (I did.) But now I'm like the girl who cried wolf, cried dog, cried so much and so many times, I could not be believed. I don't cry wolf, I don't cry tears. I open my mouth and someone else does all of whatever is done.

She is behind me, underneath. I'm on her lap and hollow and her hand is up my neck, that hole. She's got her hand— it's firm and stiff—around the wooden end of my wooden tongue. It's painted black with that special spiffy waterproof paint that makes everything look shiny and wet. She's got her fist around that stump and she is tugging it, she's wagging it and saying things that I would never say.

No one can see her, only me, and only sometimes me. Then only sometimes, rarely, when I can twist my head and see her from the corner of my eye. My eye is a marble, milky edged, with pretty, curly lashes that are not mine. Sometimes my eye folds into me and all I see is dark.

I feel her breath on the back of my neck, her mouth against my hair. I think it's from a human head, but remade for a doll's. It's fine and thin and fly-away. She likes it. She presses her face against it and says hideous, terrible things. She snickers when she says them, Hold me close.

It is not just she's a ventriloquist.

I hate to have to say this for I know to even suggest such a comparison is disrespectful, a sacrilege, against the grain, the very nut, but it's the only thing that I can think of it's like: like one of those Tibetan monks, the holy, wise, old men who can sing more than one note at a time. It's something they do with their vocal chords, they split apart, can make more than one sound at once. Each one alone can sing a chord. So she, though old but hardly holy —

Though maybe I've got that wrong, too. Maybe in fact all of it. Maybe she is the voice of God, of Him on high, of Her inside, of Everything I long for. Want. Maybe the terrible way she is is it.

Perhaps she is more like them than I thought. Both old and holy, speaking, singing words, two things at once, both hideous and glorious, the one I look as if I say, the one said just to only me alone.

She is like no one else, although, perhaps she maybe is.

Perhaps someone I used to know. Perhaps someone I would but can't forget.

The Last Time I Saw You

I think the last time I saw you may have been that time near the church. I still like that church despite this though the church is also other things to me. In fact, more and more I wish I remembered those other things that are called permanent, inviolable, impregnable to assault or trespass, secure from violation or profanation, constant and true the way I remember you.

I had waited near the bridge near the church thinking you would come that way but you came another way so I didn't see you approach; you were simply there. In fact, I didn't see you approach the very first time I saw you or, now that I think about it, ever, actually. You were simply always utterly *there*. The first time I saw you I had turned a corner from the steps and you were in the hall and the midmorning light was over you and *you were radiant*. Already it had happened: I was changed. This wasn't something I thought about or that happened gradually over time; already in the instant that I saw you, it was done.

I think I thought back then that you had done it. But

now I think that maybe you didn't. Maybe it was me. Maybe it was always ever only me. Maybe you would rather have been an innocent bystander.

It was, that is to say, *I* was, perhaps I always had been, from the very first so waiting.

I had waited near the bridge near the church, I think, though I can't remember which bridge, though I can of course remember which church, thinking you would come that way but you came another way so I didn't see you approach.

But maybe you didn't come by a bridge at all.

The last time we saw each other we hadn't seen each other for months. We had been living in different countries and happened, this day, to be in the same city and managed to arrange, without anyone else knowing, to meet for a Coke or something. Coffee? Lunch? A drink? In a public place. Of course a public place. You wanted me to know, in advance, that it would be a public place so that I would not imagine or expect.

I remember waiting near the church and you came to me.

I don't remember what we said.

I don't remember where we went.

But I think we went to a rather nondescript restaurant-bar-cafe kind of place where we could get a Coke or lunch or coffee or a drink though I wouldn't have had a drink. I would not have had a drink because I was no longer drink-ing. At all. Never. Not just around you. Or rather was about to be no longer at all. That is to say, I was planning to quit which was almost just as good as, and even if I had been still at all (drinking, not waiting, I am still waiting), I certainly would not have around you because that was important. It was important to show you I had changed. As if I was no longer what you had figured out I was.

We had coffee, mine black, yours with a touch of white, as usual.

Wait—

I would have had coffee, that day at the nondescript restaurant cafe by the church, but you wouldn't have because you weren't doing coffee any more because you were on a new health thing.

Maybe we talked about the new health thing which you were hoping would work and I hoped so too. We used to hope a lot of things.

No, you were drinking a mineral water, not "bubbly" as you called it or "fuzzy" as I called it, but "still" as you called it, or "plain" as I called it. Or maybe a fresh squeezed orange juice (not grapefruit, which you can't abide, whereas I could take or leave it) because it was one of those kinds of nice healthy health food places and I had a French press coffee. Or maybe a mineral water because you were.

The place was quiet, just you and me and the the woman tidying up before the lunch rush and the hippie kid behind the shiny chrome bar, a twentyish-year-old white guy with dreads and a string of brightly colored beads around his neck and a scraggly blond beard, who was chopping his carrots and celery and beets and oranges and apples for the delicious, healthy organic vegetable and fruit juices this place specialized in. There was even a bunch of wheat grass prominently displayed on the bar and behind the bar were all the beautiful glasses that the guy was polishing, whipping his perfectly brilliantly white linen cloth around, folding it and unfolding it as crisp as the white tuxedo shirt he wore beneath his bartender's vest, his carefully unkempt-appearing designer stubble, until those beautiful lovely glasses behind the bar shone like all the stars in heaven.

I loved those glasses. All their different shapes and sizes, the little shot glasses and the brandy snifters and pints and mugs and schooners and wine glasses, different sizes for red and white, the champagne flutes and sherry glasses and highball glasses and glasses for margaritas and sidecars and manhattans, how they were stacked along in front of the mirror and hung from the overhead rack of the antique mahogany bar which looked like something out of a Western. There was nobody else in the place, just Jack the bartender and Claire the cleaning woman and that pathetic old soak at the end of bar sucking back her shots alone and completely unaware of anyone. Except she must have been, if she was a regular, which she was, in attendance at this particular watering hole bright and early every morning, so of course she was aware that there were other people in the bar, if not other customers, like you, then certainly Jack and Claire, who she saw every single day of the week, except Saturdays and Tuesdays which Claire had off, and Tuesdays and Wednesdays when Jack was off, but she didn't or wouldn't, either because she was too embarrassed or ashamed or just plain ol' self-absorbed to acknowledge anyone else by something as simple as a mere glance up, at, toward or in the direction of someone else, some small but by its mere occurrence, significant, acknowledgment of the presence in the room of other members of her species.

On the other hand, maybe she doesn't feel like she is a member of the species.

Maybe she just needs her medicinals to kick in before she can loosen up enough to mutter "hello" or "good morning" or "hhhhnnnnngggnn" to anyone. Or maybe in fact, she is already too far gone, having arrived here at 10 A.M. or 11 A.M. or whenever opening time was this time of year (daylight savings or not, I can't decide), having previously fortified herself at home in front of the early morning TV news with a couple of slugs in her instant coffee (black), to be aware any longer of anything at all going on outside her skull. Or maybe the fact is that by this point in her, what in other circumstances might be called "life," she is so quasi-permanently fogged that she really and truly has no idea there is another living fucking soul in the fucking room.

Or maybe she's just shy.

In any event, there she was, this miserable cow, quietly sucking back her hooch as she does every day of her "life," the better part of which is spent on her very own personal and for all intents and purposes, reserved, bar stool, already soused and already doused in some putrid and unconvincing "perfume" and already having chewed an assortment of breath mints Rolaids or Tums before leaving her bachelorette apartment in the childish belief that no one would be able to smell the sweet and sour boozy perma-stink that oozes out of her that everyone can.

You and I were at our corner table talking quietly. The door was open and the sun was coming in, the bright clear mid-morning sun, and Claire was stepping outside to sweep by the front door, and I could see her shadow, sweeping the front steps in front of the bar, and hear the traffic, buses squeaking and the hiss and deflate of air brakes, cars stopping and starting at corners, little uniformed boys yelling on their way to the swanky private school across the courtyard, car radios, guys selling newspapers, the gal at the establishment one door down throwing a bucket of water on the sidewalk and sweeping it clean. I loved how clean everything smelled (except the miserable old soak, of course, but let's not go into that again). I remember that light, that beautiful clean pure heavenly churchy light, milky and thick and honey colored with golden specks of dust in it, each speck, each little tiny speck as if an entire universe, a spinning jewel, a sparkling gem, each brilliant, glowing, shining, its own little sun, collapsing, falling and leaving no trace, no earthly trace, no one will know, well maybe someone, but maybe not, and the silhouette of Claire sweeping, her sturdy working woman's arms and legs, her ropy neck, the way the sunlight came through where her sleeve hung from her arm—she was wearing a flower print dress, a scalloped apron—and the way she swung the broom, balletic, firm, an arc, a dip, the sound it made, soothing, hushed, then, once, how she stopped her beautiful beautiful sweeping and held her broom away from her body with one hand—I heard the bristles stop and stand—then lifted her other hand, her left, to her brow to block the beautiful creamy buttery yellow sun from her eyes and shout a friendly "hello!" to Bill at the flower stall across the way. Then something about Bill's daughter because both of their daughters — a couple of dolls, I tell you, young and sweet and bouncy and eager as puppies, the way people can be before the crap of the world frappées itself into their innocent unsuspecting but extremely corruptible brains — were on some school team together growing and their team winning something. They sounded everyday and kind. They sounded, Bill and Claire, for this mid-morning moment, happy.

But maybe we didn't meet there.

Maybe we went to a bar. Maybe the bar I took you to the first time you came to visit me and that was so, as you said, "eye opening" though also, as you also said, "quite normal-seeming." Or maybe we met at one of those cheap little Italian places I loved so much that you had never been to before and grew to love. You really loved those places, how noisy and crowded and close they were, how, as you often used to say "so alive!" Which you also said about me: "You're so alive!" Or maybe we went to one of those health food type places your doctor recommended when you were starting to get ill or maybe we walked along the river.

Maybe we sat on a bench beneath a big wide tree and looked out at the river and got some bread and fed the ducks which you also always loved to do after we did it the first time.

I couldn't believe the things you hadn't done before and you couldn't either. You said you were seeing a whole new world, a whole new you.

You said you were becoming who you were always meant to be.

I don't know whether I really believed you or whether I only wanted to.

Maybe we watched the boats going out and talked about how far away things get before one realizes and by then it's too late.

Maybe we went back to the cabin where we'd spent the week that summer when you said to me the things you said and I said them back to you, and then after we had done the things — you wanted to do them too, you asked — and then the things you did not know, but I did, and when I did them you held me and wept and held me and told me Yes.

But I don't think we went back to the cabin. I would remember that.

Maybe we met at that nondescript place by the church except a little later in the day. Maybe it was closer to lunchtime. Maybe it was just as the lunch crowd was arriving and that old pathetic stinking soak at the bar was about to push off and head home — alone, of course, because everything about her was alone, cut off, removed, separate, eviscerated from whatever she thought she should have been a part of, disemboweled from what she had, prematurely perhaps, but nonetheless quite fixedly attached herself to, before being amputated from the "life" she, without much reason, actually, had decided she ought to have because she had waited for it, her whole fucking life she had waited for it, that had either made her, or at least given her an excuse to say had made her turn into the pathetic maudlin morbid stinking self-absorbed vicious old wreck she was who sometimes, honest to god, could barely keep herself from shitting in her pants, an embarrassment, a parasite, a bygod crying shame because once, it's true, one time the poor girl had actually had a lot of "potential" (what a waste)—for her afternoon "nap" (read: blackout) before she returned back to the semi-dumpy but lovable place for her pre-happy hour drink which would be followed by her happy hour drinks then her post-happy hour drinks after which she would spend the entire evening doing post post-happy hour drinks until closing when Mike, the night barman, or one of the college girls who cycled through the place (Claire having gotten off work at 3 to meet her kids when they came home from school and get ready for the ever ongoing cribbage tournament she'd been playing with Stewie and Marty and Ange for the last who can remember how many years) would walk the poor cow home.

The poor cow would be pushing off for her "nap" now because she hated the noisy young lunch crowd which reminded her how everything's so different from the way things used to be from what she had once hoped or wanted or sometimes even almost expected but now didn't like to be reminded of now because she didn't like how things had turned out.

Not that she always liked to remember how things were.

I mean, she did, often, actually most of the time, when she was conscious, not dozing or in a blackout, *remember* things. But she didn't always *like* to remember. Or rather not *every*thing. That is, she liked to remember only *some* things, *some* of the ways things used to be, but not the other ways because the other ways were awful. Some things had really turned out quite awfully, what with all the shouting and crying and break-ing of crockery and late night phone fights and late night, uh, uh, reconciliations, and slamming of doors and slamming of heads and changings of locks then changings of addresses, etc., etc., sometimes to places as far away as other countries.

In fact, some things had turned out awfully, miserably, worse than she, than either of them in their wildest imaginations, nightmares, dreams or vengeance fantasies, could have imagined. And one of them, we gather, could imagine quite alot.

But she also remembered, and often liked to remember, the times that were, and she believed there were many, actually good. Yes. For also there were times of being glad.

But almost as soon as she remembered these times that had been good and/or glad, she also remembered that these times had not lasted. So the remembering of good times would also make her miserable and maudlin. The problem, that is, *one* of the problems, and of course there were many, was that it was hard to remember only one kind of time (i.e. a "good" time) without the other kind of time (i.e. a "bad" time) because they were so intertwined, the good with the bad, the joyful with the terrible, the radiant with the horrible. She could not separate them in her mind which was the only place they existed anymore.

Though, to be entirely honest, there were at least *some*-times when she could remember only some of the things that had been, or at least seemed for a while to be, good.

Whereas now very little was. Now there was very little reason to try at all. To be at all. I mean, honestly.

If someone were to give her a reason, one good reason, it doesn't have to be a big reason, a little one would do, she might listen. But no one did.

Or maybe someone did but she didn't listen.
As also she had not listened times before.

She had come to think that there was no reason to stick around at all so why not just spend the rest of her "life" on a barstool in some godforsaken dive until somebody sweeps her, along with the dirt and crap and cigarette butts and twisted up linty snot-and tear-soaked Kleenexes and tops of lipstick thingies and ticket stubs and condom packages and chewing gum wrappers and sticky unidentified crap, out into the street at the end of the day?

Maybe you and I were lucky enough to get wherever we did—cafe? restaurant? holding pen? bar?—before the lunch run and actually get our table, which they were also kind enough to try to keep for us, because it actually was kind of a spiffy lunch place, not nondescript or dumpy, where bankers and lawyers and broker types ate, in which case we would have had lunch, but I don't remember that or more importantly, I can't imagine that because that was not the kind of place we used to go to. But maybe we went there precisely because it was the kind of place we didn't go to, except on special occasions, and therefore we would be able to compartmentalize the memory of whatever we said and did not say and what we did and did not do in an effort to keep separate from the other memories the memory of this last time we would see each other which you knew it was.

You would have thought of that.

I wouldn't have. I still had hope.

I would have wanted to go back to someplace we had

been together a lot before in order to bring back all the times we had been together.

I would have wanted to make you reconsider, again, what you had already reconsidered many times.

You had given the chance that I had asked for. You had given me many chances. You held out longer than anybody should.

I was the one who didn't do what I said. I was the one who lied.

The last time we met, we met in a place that was quiet and slow because we were going to talk.

I don't remember what we said. I do remember me begging, again, for something.

Maybe I begged you for something you could not give. Maybe I begged for what nobody can. Maybe I tried again — and whether I was trying to tell the truth or whether I was lying, I still don't know — to tell you you were wrong about me.

But maybe that time I finally stopped pretending.

Maybe, that time, I admitted you were right. Maybe I said that I knew I had been kidding myself but that I still wasn't going to do what I needed to do because I was a coward and a liar and afraid and that I knew that I had stolen something from you like a thief. And maybe I cannot bear to have said what I said, what I might have said, and to know that it is true. Maybe I cannot bear for you to know what you know about me. I cannot bear to know that you loved me once and look what I did to you.

Aspects of the Novel

E.M. Forster delivered the talks (the Clark lectures) that turned into his book *Aspects of the Novel* to a bunch of Cambridge undergrads in the spring of 1927. Cambridge was then, and I hope still is now, a fey little island of gay male beauty. (Male indeed. Virginia Woolf also lectured on literature to females at Newnham and Girton women's colleges at Cambridge in 1928 during which time the standing of the female students was secondary. Comparatively crappy dorms, comparatively crappy food, etc. The men, nice as their surroundings were, were locked in wherever they were . . . Woolf wrote about all of this in *A Room of One's Own*). I imagine a slew, a riot, a river (the Granta? I think . . . this place having only ever been a place of fantasy to me, a place of envy, a place for others) an ocean, a country house, a regiment, a stable, a gardener hut, a sailor bar, a bevy full of pretty privileged boys in starched white uniform shirts, open collared, slightly déshabillé, their slightly musty (the English don't wash) hair scented of oil, hanging into and over their blue, green and deep brown, doe brown eyes, their long thick eyelashes . . . and their delicate white skinned ink stained blue veined hands, their pink chapped lips, little sticks of dry flesh sticking up that one might want to pull off with one's teeth or press down with his tongue, their trembling fingers reaching grasping stretching picking fondling toward . . . uh . . . toward . . . uh . . . uh . . . that which toward is reached.

(Her hair was black, her eyes were grey. Her skin, her hands were white. There was the light in the hall. There was the window. It was autumn. It was the morning and there was the rustle of everyone else. They were all in uniform. White shirt. Green wool. Sensible shoes. Hair falling unkempt, untidy but not hers. Hers was always perfect as always she always was.)

A novel is a thing that's made. Created. Hewn. Invented. Never happened.

(It never happened.)

Only secondarily, if at all, is it "realistic" or "representative" or "accurate" or "honest" or any of those unthought through words that are tossed around these days like so much confetti like so much snow. Doesn't anybody think about what they say anymore? Doesn't anybody think that someone may be listening? That someone may believe? Some poor miserable cuss.

(As if a light surrounding her. As if in snow. Except I can't remember if it ever did or didn't when I saw her, snow. It might have. It might have not.

Maybe confetti's the closest it ever got. If that and even if, each piece so small, in another context trash, as glamourous as dandruff. Detritus.)

Forster had written many novels before he gave the lectures to the white skinned boys at Cambridge with their musty breath, the smell inside their shirts, their shiny smooth and hairless chests, swimmers' chests and so forth that became *Aspects of the Novel*.

(The whiteness of her stomach. The way the muscles in her stomach flexed. The sweat on the back of her neck. The way the bottom of her hair was wet in points. The slip of wet. The stick of salt.)

In 1927 Forster was forty-eight years old and had published, to increasing esteem, a slew of novels including: *Where Angels Fear to Tread* (1905); *A Room With a View* (1908); *Howard's End* (1910) and, in 1924, the great, grand, true, wise and loving *A Passage to India*. (Forster had traveled to India in 1912 with Goldsworthy Lowes Dickinson, a typical Cambridge don, who, among other things, enjoyed being trodden upon by booted young men.)

(There were those whole lotta years between us. How long had you waited? How stupid were you? How repressed? How stupid was I? Am I? How dogged, how immovable? How out of grace? How unforgiving? Of anyone. You or me.)

Which sadly brings us to the tragic or rather, *a* tragic part, of Forster's life as a writer which is the fact that *A*

Passage to India was the last novel he wrote. Forster went on to write and publish a great many things—essays, biography, stories—until his death in 1970. But he never wrote or published another novel after 1924.

How come?

(I still don't get it sometimes. Sometimes I think I do.)

In chapter III of *Aspects of the Novel*,[1] Forster says this:

"Since the novelist is himself a human being, there is an affinity between him and his subject matter which is absent from many other forms of art."

(Though some are more than others. Maybe not every one is a human being. Maybe some do not deserve the name. Maybe some of us ought to be put away for our own and our environment's well being. Maybe some of us do not deserve to breathe. But also aren't worth, as my mother used to say, "the dynamite it would take to blow you up."

NB: *I do not wish to suggest that any of this was in any way at all her (my mother's) fault. My mother was a very good human being, decent and kind, and she worked very hard and gave us all she could.*

I don't know where in Jesus' name I ever came from.

She didn't deserve what happened.)

I'm going to put aside the question of whether the novel really has more room for biographical/personal affinity between itself and its maker than other forms of art. The important thing here is that the novel was *Forster's* form of art. When we was talking about "the novelist," he was talking about himself. He was telling us that there was an important affinity between himself and the subjects, or rather, I should say, subject, (singular) because the more I read him the more I think his novels were all about the same subject.

(You don't understand, she said, I can't. It isn't possible. I can't. It would destroy me.

Then later and, apparently to her though not to me, unrelated: She calls me from Cambridge every day. Every single day she calls me from Cambridge.

The phone rang and I left the room. I should have known. I did know. I knew all along. Why was I kidding myself?)

In the introductory chapter of *Aspects of the Novel* Forster says this:

"The final test of the novel will be our affection for it, as it is the test of our friends, and of anything else which we cannot define."

(Where affection came from:
Affect 1: 1) to have an effect upon; influence
*   2) to move or stir the emotions*
Affect 2: 1) to like to have, use, wear, etc.
*   2) to pretend to have, feel, like, etc. feign.*
Affectation: 2) artificial behavior meant to impress others.
Affected: 1) attacked by disease
*   3) emotionally moved*
Affection: 1) a tendency or disposition
*   3) a disease: ailment* [2]

Was I a final test of you? Were you the test of me? Did I ever give you half a chance? Or did I stack the deck? Did I from day one, from the first, stack us against us? The greatest test, the final time, you said you never would. You did not then but did eventually. Did I ever have a chance? I don't remember. I don't remember what I want. I wonder if you don't remember too.)

For Forster, the ultimate test of the novel is not its shape or its gravity, not its invention or its social importance, but our personal response to it. How it "affects" or moves us. This can be emotional, it can be physical. A thing that gives you shivers, puts you into tears, makes you embarrassed and glad that there is no one else in the room with you to see you flushed or blushing, to see you angry, hopeless, exhausted and ridiculous with tears and snot, red-faced and hiccuping and spitty. These responses cannot be argued as much as experienced. One cannot help it. One is swept up in it. *(So we were swept and then so wept.)* This ultimate test can be uncomfortable, indefensible. As uncomfortable and indefensible as love.

Forster wrote a lot about love. It was his subject: how we are and are not allowed to love in the cultures in which we live. How our desires and our varieties and forms of love can both destroy us and redeem us.

(I am waiting to be redeemed. I am always waiting something.)

Forster's work as a novelist was both destroyed and redeemed by love.

Of the many aspects—biographical, aesthetic, social—that contributed to what he wrote as a novelist, the greatest of these was Love.

(Rhymes with "shove." Meaning obvious. And "glove." As in, "if it doesn't fit don't wear it." And "of." As in "You are out of your mind."

Perhaps that was a cause. NB: I say "a" not "the" because I am kind enough to suggest that there were several things that trapped you, that made you do what you said you "had" to do blah blah blah rather than just saying right out what I think from time to time, that being that you were just a coward and a liar.

What you are now?)

A Passage to India was the last novel Forster wrote and the last novel published during his lifetime. But the year after Forster died, in 1970, his novel, *Maurice*, was published. *Maurice* had been completed in 1914, when Forster was already regarded as one of the major novelists in England. But Forster held *Maurice* back from publication because of its homosexual content. I have the somewhat sinking feeling that these days probably more people have seen the movie than have read the book. I guess that's not so bad. I thought it was a pretty good movie. Like that dear scene where they first touch, so tender, so tentative. Hugh Grant was actually pretty good, believe it or not.

And I usually — let me rephrase that: I always otherwise if not hate, no hate is too big a word, I know what hate is and this is not that. Rather I am annoyed with his calculated bluster, his cute hapless boy, privileged rich kid faux blunder. I mean, honestly, how hard can life be for anyone as good looking and rich as that? I wish I could key his fabulous shiny new car or break the windows in his house or throw eggs at him or steal his girlfriend or something. I find it very hard to feel even remotely sorry for people like that.

Where was I?

(Where was I in your life? I know so well, for I remember everything, where I was when I knew you in your house and in your town and in your bed and in your car and in your office in your bed the stairwell in your pants your mouth your bed oh in your grace.)

I am glad that a movie with gay content could have become such a part of our popular culture. I am also glad that I live when I do, rather than when poor Forster did. Which brings me back to Forster's history and why he wrote what he did when he did and stopped writing what he did when he did. Why he was able, in the 1920's and beyond, to talk openly, wisely, generously (though I disagree with him about Stein) about many aspects of the novel but, sadly denied himself, or was denied, the ability to publish a novel that talked about the most passionate and pleasured aspects of himself.

By 1914, when Forster had finished writing *Maurice*, though men who had sex with other men were no longer punished by hanging (as had been made the law in Britain in 1533), men known to commit homosexual acts could still lose their jobs, their homes, their careers. (Lesbians, comparatively, did not exist—what else is new?—legally, criminally. Invisibility has had its uses. Also its costs . . .) In 1861 capital punishment for sodomy was outlawed, only to be replaced by life imprisonment, until, in 1885, the sentence for sodomy or "gross indecency" was reduced to two years hard labor. (The "gross indecency" thing was what they got Oscar Wilde with in 1895.) As late as 1952 1,686 men in Britain were prosecuted for "gross indecency" (i.e. homosexual behavior) and were punished by being forced to undergo chemical castration. In other words, Forster had good reasons for wanting to keep his homosexuality a secret.

(I also find it hard to feel sorry for people who have a goddamn choice. I mean, it may be all well and good if you do but most people don't. Most people just plain don't. Some people don't have anything.

On the other hand, you always said, well, not always actually, early on you said just the opposite, you said you would, you were, it was and it would be. But later you always, that is often, said, "You don't understand. I don't have a choice."

But I did understand.

And you did have a choice, goddammit.

You just chose not to take it.)

In 1922, Forster wrote this in his diary: "Having at this moment burnt my indecent writings or as many as the fire will take. Not a moral repentance, but the belief that they clogged me artistically. They were written not to express myself but to excite myself, and when first—15 years back?—I began them, I had a feeling that I was doing something positively dangerous to my career as a novelist . . ." (April 8, 1922.)[3]

(Indecent to excite oneself? Indecent to be excited? Hardly. Consider, at the most base level, the need for the species to replicate itself. No, rather, what is indecent is to lie.

I wrote to myself, Never, Never again.

I wrote it again and again.

I wrote it every time I did again and every time I said that I would not again because it would kill me, it really would, but then I did it again and it didn't. I don't know why. I don't know why the fuck I am still alive. Is this someone's idea of a joke?)

Forty years later, in 1964, Forster wrote this in his diary: "I should have been a more famous writer if I had written more or rather published more, but sex has prevented the latter." (December 31, 1964. Please note, this is New Year's Eve. The poor old guy, in his mid-eighties at the time, was looking back over his year, his life, and regretting what he did and did not do.)

(Regret can last forever.)

Please note here too, the distinction Forster makes between what he has "written" and what he has "published."

Of course we can't know what Forster set fire to back when he was in his 40's, but we can know he knew it would be dangerous to his career as a novelist.

Even so, he was daring enough, in 1928, to write a letter of support for the socially important (though stylistically awful) writer Radclyffe Hall when she was put on trial for obscenity following the publication of her plea-in-the-form-of-a-novel for the understanding of female "inverts," *The Well of Loneliness.* *(Have any of you fuckers ever heard of fucking mercy?)* Forster and his queer, gay, lesbian, invert, bi, alienated affectionate elite, whatever you want to call most of the Bloomsbury gang, did what they could to try to change the world into one in which they could write what they wanted to write without fear of censorship or imprisonment. But it took a while.[4]

In the meantime, the inability to write openly as a man who loved his own kind took a toll on Forster. Here's something he confessed to his diary in 1911:

"Having sat for an hour in vain trying to write a play, I will analyze the causes of my sterility . . . 2. Weariness of the only subject that I both can and may treat—the love of men for women and vice versa." (Diary, June 16, 1911).

1911 was still early in his working life, but he was already feeling "sterile" because he had resigned himself to the fact that the only subject he could treat publicly in his novels was "the love of men for women and vice versa." Fortunately, he could not stop himself from writing about the love of men for men.

(Maybe we were not each other's kind. Maybe you were right.)
Within a couple of years of when he wrote this in his diary, Forster was also secretly working on *Maurice*.

Fast forward to 1927: Forster is a pudgy, ever more softening graying middle aged homosexual delivering the Clark lectures to a bevy of lovely Cambridge boys. *(Greying, pudgy middle aged homosexual. Bevy of pretty, breathless, by virtue of their cluelessness, willing, eager, awestruck students of similar inclination: Pick me! Pick me!)* While Forster, who has his literary chops down as much as anyone, can go on intelligently about the relationship between Poetry and History, James and Richardson, Dickens and Wells, the relationship between the Women's Movement and fiction in nineteenth century Britain, he is less interested in writing about the relationship of the novel to any historical chronology than to what it says about the interior life.

(Where most of the lives of this particular variety of miserable human being or not occur.)
In the "People" chapter of *Aspects of the Novel*, Forster writes: "A memoir is history, it is based on evidence. A novel is based on evidence + pr—x, the unknown quality being the temperament of the novelist, and the unknown quantity always modifies the effect of the evidence, and sometimes transforms it entirely.

"The historian deals with actions . . . He is as much concerned with character as the novelist, but he can only know its existence when it shows on the surface."

(The evidence of who you were was me.)

Forster knew a lot about the "unknown . . . temperament of the novelist." He knew that he could never publicly reveal the things he felt inside himself. He knew a lot about the difference between surface appearance and things that do not appear on the surface. He knew a lot about what he calls "the hidden life":

"The hidden life is, by definition, hidden . . . And it is the function of the novelist to reveal the hidden life at its source."

(The only evidence of you was me.

If it would be revealed. But it would not.

Who were you really trying to hide from? Who were you really trying to hide? What was in me that hid itself in you?)

Forster's own hidden life was a life in which he loved men passionately, not only the pretty privileged undergrads to whom he was delivering his lecture, but also to men of the "lower classes." (In a diary entry of 1935 Forster wrote: "I want to love a strong young man of the lower classes and be loved by him and even hurt by him." Forster knew all sorts of reasons to hide this part of his life. He took up with a policeman late in his life.)

You can almost hear Forster sadly bidding his work as a novelist adieu during his Clark Lectures. A couple pages after the passages cited above, he laments the following:

"In daily life we never understand each other . . . We know each other approximately, by external signs. . . . But people in a novel can be understood completely by the reader, if the novelist wishes; their inner as well as their outer life can be exposed. And this is why they often seem more definite than characters in history or even our own friends; we have been told all about them that can be told; even if they are imperfect or unreal they do not contain secrets, whereas our friends do and must, mutual secrecy being one of the conditions of life upon this globe."

(I wanted to break through all of that. I wanted to tell and hear and you wanted to tell me too and so you did. I was the only one who heard, the only one you told and though you tried to forget I didn't. I can't. I won't for both. A secret is a thing that we hold dear. This secret is the thing that holds us, dearie, still.)

What strikes me here so sharply, so sadly is Forster's admission that a novelist can—therefore should?—expose the inner life. Forster suggests a kind of ideal knowingness between the novel and its writer. But he is not able, given the social era and his temperament, to write a *publishable* novel that reveals his own inner life too directly. It's not a coincidence that his novels are full of ingenue girls who find love that their society regards as improper with dark, handsome working or "lower" class men in foreign countries.

(Digits and weeping. Fluid and tears. Whimpering noises and turning away.)

Aspects of the Novel was, and remains, an intelligent, savvy study of the British novel up to the modernist movement. But *Aspects of the Novel* was also, when it was delivered in 1927, a swan song, an admission from a gay writer that he could no longer write the kinds of novels he wanted to write for publication. He couldn't risk revealing his hidden life. He could only ever refer to it, which he did for the rest of his life, by hidden clues.

Adieu, my love! Adieu, adieu, adieu!

Notes:

The stuff about gay history is mostly from *Completely Queer: The Gay and Lesbian Encyclopedia*, by Steve Hogan and Lee Hudson, Henry Holt, 1998.

1) page 44 of the edition I am reading: *Aspects of the Novel*, Harcourt, Brace Harvest paperback, 1955, the year before I was born.

2) These definitions are taken from *Webster's New World Dictionary, Second Concise Edition*. I am still using an edition from 1982. I find it very hard to let go of the past.

3) Thanks to Oliver Stallybrass for his terrific introduction to *The Life to Come and Other Stories*, Avon, 1972, three years after the Stonewall riots, two years after the death of Forster, (if only he'd been younger) from whence I get a lot of the quotations from Forster's diaries and letters.

4) You can read a good narrative of what all happened with Woolf et al trying to rally around Hall in Hermione Lee's great biography, *Virginia Woolf*, Knopf, 1977. You can also read here, or lots of other places about Woolf's own lesbian romance fantasy, *Orlando*, composed and published in the 1920's.

A romance and a fantasy that was.

Enough

I cannot have how I want.
   I could perhaps the human way like any body can, but that is not enough.

I want entirely.

I can't really imagine this. I mean, I'm capable of imagining a lot but there's a way that what one can imagine could, if one imagines properly, occur. This can't.

But want will not undo itself.

Therefore I see an opening and I am helped by something pulling in.

I can imagine what I've seen.

Then what I haven't. Although not easily, not quite without effort, although I know how things are born, the opening canal, the light—then I can see.

I long to be inside how is not possible.

Or only is so in my head where what has never can.

Perhaps I've only ever partly lived
or was not fully born
so long to go back where I never partly left.

Now, in my head, I am inside and both of us are holding both our breath.

My surface has not felt like this before. Although perhaps it has but can't remember, perhaps before it was, to whatever degree I was or wasn't, born. It feels matted like something swimming, an otter, a seal, a dolphin with fur, except the fur is swept backwards like the arm of the vet up the hole of a cow with a calf calving upside down. Perhaps I, too, was born like that, bent backwards, my direction wrong, not wanting to go out but back.

Then I am inside, further in. I know this is impossible. Not to mention the punch line of a zillion stupid jokes.

However.

I feel like I am swimming, pulling, the breaststroke or the butterfly, stretching slowly like in a movie, like a drop of something viscous, molasses, maple syrup, water, oil as it collects and gathers, bulges, lengthens, thins then is released.

Then I am further deeper in, I will not surface, will not stop, but further where the rocks are slick, my hands are slipping over them, the water dark, and I can hide and feel the movements of the things I almost see. I'm almost there with both my hands, but also I am almost out of breath, but I don't want to leave, I won't, my lungs about to burst but I won't stop, I'd rather die. I feel, in fact like I am almost dying, shot, my head is pressing, something shoots —

Then it isn't up to me. There's Something else that brings me up.

I shoot out in the air and sputter light.

Except, I'm still inside there too.

Though I remember being here, I don't remember going. Was it like a crowning backwards? The top of my head would have felt it first, like the water sprinkled for baptism. Except it is like nothing else I know.

Miraculously, like one of those dreams I have of breathing underwater, I'm breathing here inside and we are both of us alive.

Then it's different. I'm no longer coming up, but rather between what's like a seam right down the middle like in one of those thick, plastic oval coin purses that one squeezes open from top to bottom. Or maybe it's like there's a zipper from the bottom of your stomach to the bottom of your neck and I have come in from there and I am in the soft insides. I feel this all with all of me with skin and hands and blood. In fact, there's blood all over everywhere. It smells the rich, metallic way it tastes. It tastes like I am breathing it, but we are not in danger. There is no hemorrhage or wound. No, rather, it's like we are both inside some ultra thin, see-through plastic wrap, though not thoroughly impermeable because some of it does get on and in me which is not only necessary but also very nice. Or perhaps it is more like one of those crinkly bread wrappers with all those little teeny holes. There is a hum, a pulse and swishing sounds, things opening and coursing. Warm as milk.

I am not alone in here.

I am in here with you.

You're smaller now, the size of me.

Did I forget to mention that I've shrunk?

And the amazing thing is this doesn't bother the big you outside at all! The big you outside doesn't feel queasy or sick the way one might if there were some thing, two things actually, crawling around inside. It also doesn't look from the outside like there's a couple of lumps or growths or rather, insofar as we stick so close together, one thing or things. In fact, it looks almost normal, at most a bulge or thickening about which others might think, How sweet!

We slip around so easily inside. Like a couple of kids in the snow (do you remember that?) except it's warm. As milk. Actually we're more like a couple of kids on one of those Slippy Slides that I remember from when I was a kid. Do you remember that?

The way, though dark and thick, is clear. There is a breath, a pause, a pull and I am pulled toward, am almost near enough, not quite, to reach the thing I came here for: *I want to hold your heart.*

Consolation

We were not consolable.

We lowered our heads and blew our noses and wrung our hands. We signed papers, paid bills, moved furniture, cleaned rooms then cleaned other stuff that actually didn't need cleaning. We twittered around. We ate too much then not enough. We slept too much then not enough. We started smoking again (though, fortunately, this did not last.) We went on and on and on but we did not "get better in time." We did not get over it.

We were told we needed help.

The experts were called in.

They came and though they all, though perhaps not in this order for they began to run together in our minds, tried. The woman in the loose dark dresses with long gray hair and many billowy silky ethnic scarves and bracelets and necklaces who often kept her eyes closed when she spoke, for although she told us frequently there was "nothing to be said" she said a whole, whole lot and did so softly (frequently), fiercely (frequently), breathily, dramatically, (would-be) sexily, overbearingly, talking and talking and talking then doing what she called "ritual work" that at first merely surprised and puzzled but then actually embarrassed us, though it also gave us moments of surreptitious levity. (Remind me some time to tell you about the time she channeled someone named Theozone for us.) We were unbelievably polite through all of this, well, most of this. We did not lose our manners. We did not tell her how embarrassing she was. (By the way, if I ever get anywhere near behaving like that, please shoot me. In fact feel free, at any time, to shoot me. Please.) There was the soft skinned young man, prematurely bald, who spoke softly and with his soft white palms opened upward, as if he could comfort or catch or hold some one of us, but he could not. Though some of us were fond of how he tried. He was sincere. There were the women with terrible senses of rhythm with drums, (another if-ever-I please shoot me), the fire walking men, the long haired ponytailed old white guy, the chanting man, the feathered guy, the boys who sang like angels, the fully grown adults who spoke of angels, then of aliens, of martians, Raeleans, Druids, the Chariots of the Gods people and Rosicrucians, often in words they couldn't pronounce, of *olde*, with an "e," *anciente* with an "e" *thinges* with an "es," which was how they spelled them, and gave us their web addresses. There were the chatty ones and the (almost) silent ones. There were the jokey ones. ("Dead guy walks into a bar . . .") There was the one with the perfect hair and perfect teeth, a fabulous tan and an even more fabulous alimony settlement who spoke about how "we bring nothing to ourselves that we don't really desire for our own personal destiny." This one did, actually, try our patience. To the tune that some of us had to hold some of the others of us back from doing what some of us would have liked to do to her by extremely politely saying, "Excuse me, but I need to share with you I don't feel like this, uh, your, uh, personal truth is uh working for us . . ." There were the therapy pets and Mr. HappySad, the hospital clown, and there was even the guy from the gym. There was the friend with the frequent flyers miles for the faraway exotic trip of a "lifetime" (though also he said, after he had said it, that that was probably not the best way to have said it). They each, well, most, to varying degrees were well-intentioned, earnest, kind. (Except for that bitch with the perfect teeth.) People, that is, *many* people are kind. They really are! They were—and alas also are—utterly useless.

At least to us. Which we said to them. Because we didn't want them to feel bad (except for the perfect toothed bitch. We'd have liked her to feel bad. We'd have liked her to feel like she was shitting razor blades. Then we would have liked to hear her explain how she had called this particular ass-ripping destiny down upon herself.) But we didn't want the kind, earnest, well-intentioned others to feel that they had not been able to make us feel better through any fault or deficiency of their own. So we said to them we are only us and probably just funny, not funny as in ha-ha, but funny as in fucked up.

We continued to bow our heads blow our noses wring our hands then after this had gone on far, far too long, beat our hands then our heads then our brains, well, not literally our brains because we couldn't without some kind of device, machine or assistance, like some burly dude with a black leather mask over his face and a Cro Magnon club sledge hammer ax or mallet, some extra from some movie with a guillotine or torture or SM scene or a snuff film, but we did think about how we could get rid of our incessant remembering brains. We thought if only we could beat our relentless annoying remembering brains to pulp, or put a bullet through them, or drop them and the soon to be carcass that had carried them off a forty story building into rush hour traffic, or even without traffic, because really, the effect would be the pretty much the same, traffic or no traffic, or stuff them into a meat grinder dump them in a toxic dump or sand blast them, if only we had the guts to blow them out and therefore get over it or at least get *ourselves* over with, that might be just the ticket.

But we didn't.

We attempted, instead, to turn our brains to mush interiorly. We listened to loud obnoxious screamer music and soft sweet soothing music that did not soothe. We drank like fish ate like pigs humped like bunnies like there was no tomorrow. We danced 'til dawn put lampshades on our heads crammed ourselves into fast cars traveled to exotic locales and did extreme sports. We consumed weird stuff.

Then, after an even long, long longer time, after which we really, *really* should have gotten over it, we only slowed down a little bit but basically still kept going on like the Energizer bunny.

Because none of it
not any of it
in any way shape or form
helped.

Perhaps it did not help, we began to realize, because we did not want to be "helped."

We did not want to "understand, accept, embrace or live graciously with" what had happened.

Because what had happened was terrible. It was really, really bad. It was therefore correct we should both be and feel miserable.

We did not want to be consoled.

What we wanted was for what had happened to have not happened.

In fact, we wanted more.

We wanted things to be different. We thought, to be brutally honest because the more it went the more brutally fucking honest we became, that the way things were was horrible. Immoral. Indecent. Wrong.

To have things like that "have to" happen. Why "have to"? Why not *not* have to? Why not some other way? Surely there were, or could be, other ways.

Surely Someone, anyone with even half a goddamn brain, could figure out some other way for things to be.

It was a shitty way to run a universe.

Whose idea was it, anyway, to do things like that? Huh? Whose big fat fucking idea was that?

(Long pause.)

Whose . . . Um . . . Hello? . . . Um . . . Anybody up there?

(Long pause.)

Hello? Hello?

(Long pause.)

It did not change. It was the way it was and is and evermore shall be so help us all.

We can put up or shut up.

Our consolation is not to be had.

The House

I went back to the house.

I was near the town which I rarely was so it was a chance to go back so I took it. I took the bus. I sat alone in the front of the bus and looked out the window as if I was preparing for something grand, a day I would remember. Although remembering, of course, was not the problem. Forgetting was. In that I could or would not although perhaps maybe if I went back I might if not forget at least remember differently.

Or maybe if I went back I could after all this time finally really actually truly try to get over it.

But maybe it wasn't a question of trying. Maybe it wasn't a thing I could do. Maybe it was a thing of its own and nothing I or one or anyone could do would undo it. Even you.

Maybe you had known this when you left.

I went back to the house. Where I had been before where you had waved to me. Your hand was in the window and I waited and I stood below and think I saw you wave. I believe I remember what you did though I did not know what you meant which could have been: Goodbye Come back Don't Leave Come back I will.

And so I have.

This time I went as if it might be possible to there undo or alter finish or complete an end I'd not been able to before.

Though maybe I could have then but didn't want to. Or maybe I couldn't have then but I could now. But maybe I didn't want to ever because if I did then what would be left?

Not much.

I went back as a visitor which I suppose I always was. The other people on the bus were visitors shopping. That's why people went there. I didn't used to see that I thought.

Though part of the town appeared the same even that part too seemed or was less, an ordinarily corrupted place whereas when I was there before because of and with you it was or seemed different. As if a place as if no other, as if illuminated, radiant or limned with light or something like mistaken for or similar to light as if suggesting splendor, something good and true and possible, as if it was that which would so and endlessly remain.

As opposed to a place I had to leave then you. (Doctor's orders.)

I went back after you had left.

I can't go where you went.

I didn't remember the name of the street. I didn't know how to get there. I think I was assuming, according to this idea I had of myself, that "my body would remember" as though it was burned inside of me as if a mark a scar a brand, a reconfiguration of the very synapses the way they say about babies who listen to Mozart in the womb or rats' brains that get shaped differently when their parents have had to go through mazes over and over and over, so I would know in some deep true visceral interior place my way back to the house (like riding a bike) which would also then make everything, the ways and places and years and people and everything of my life between then and now merely "like a dream" because the house and all it was was there, remaining always as it was, merely waiting for me to come back like a prince with a kiss for everything to be, again, forever as it was. But it was not.

I couldn't even remember the name of the street.

I had to get a map.

Not even a real or a detailed map. Just a freebie one with the shops banks restaurants hotels and other businesses one would patronize as a visitor, a shopper, who came for the arcades, covered malls, charmingly designed faux olde shoppes, boutiques of fancy clothes, nice shoes, the Italian restaurant, music store, Indian restaurant, Starbucks, other Starbucks, etc. Not the kind of businesses I had frequented when I was there pretending we were living normally, the grocery store and post office, the hardware store, that place we got the sweet pea seeds, the place we got your daughter's bike seat, the office supply place, the place you worked and the place we met for lunch where sometimes we'd just meet there but not order anything just run home for a quick one while your daughter was away at school, your doctor's, your other doctor's and the park.

It was an ordinary park, not anything a visitor passing through would go to but I did. I did with you. I remember the night we walked around it the first time. How I wanted but did not want to go back to your house too soon because I was wondering and hoping you were too if we walked long enough and said enough and the right things, that then when we went back to your house I would not go to the guest room again I would go to your room with you.

I went to your room. It was upstairs. I remember the swish of your skirt on the stairs as I went up with you.

The bus had stopped on a normal street a short walk to the house. I walked the same way except backward that is in the reverse direction to what I had walked each day from there when I was there many times for many years, when I had woken in the house when it was grey and pink and cool outside, the air moist if not actually raining drizzly or foggy. Sometimes you forgot or almost forgot to take an umbrella and either I would put one in your hand at the door as you left or I would go to where you worked and leave it for you or be there when you finished work and we would walk together underneath it back to your house.

It wasn't actually a house.

It was more of a townhouse a row house a terrace a brownstone kind of thing though not brown but white. A beautiful white. A white I'd never seen before and never have seen since. A kind of white that sometimes looked light purple or lavender or cream colored in the light or even a kind of grey green white, depending on the weather, whether it was fog or rain or cloud for it was rarely sunny, which was fine by you, though I could have used a bit of sun, but even in the rain or fog there would be the shine of it, how it swallowed or shot back the light, reflected it like water, and made the room go from gray to white to lavender depending on the time of day or night, for we were careful. I called it a house though it was not a house which should have told me something. I still do.

When we woke in your room outside the window of your room, which was big and clear and clean and high, a wide sash window with a curtain which when it was open let in the cooling air—a billow, a coolness and swish that was not unlike the light which before had been dark, blue, velvety, like powder, an absence of sorts, as if some thing was opening, was welcoming then too as if surrounding, holding, covering, as if there were no falling away nor falling out nor falling, unless into something sweet and damp, until then with the return of light, there was the hum of cars, the sounds of people, ordinary other regular people with jobs and families which is what everyone seemed to think you were and therefore me too, within reason, going to work, the sounds of shoes on the sidewalks, clicking, the sounds of milk bottles being left, of mail being slipped into slots, of someone's radio on in the car, dogs being walked, the newspaper tossed, and children going to school as I did once.

One time when I came back I heard this sort of for I was still partly asleep or travel drugged so it was fuzzy until I heard you. You had come up to where I slept and brought me a cup of tea. The mail had arrived and you had a letter. You sat down on the foot of the bed—I felt the end of it sink, the rustle of cotton, the swish of skin—as you opened the letter. I remember the sound of the letter knife, then the swish of your hands as you slipped it out then read it to me. I couldn't decide whether to lie there with my eyes closed so I could listen to your voice or open my eyes so I could look at you. The letter was to you from me and I had beat the letter there. We looked at each other and smiled and looked— I remember the sound of you lying the letter on the bed— for we were glad.

I used the map and found the street and then when I got to the street I could not remember which house though it was not a house.

I couldn't believe I had forgotten, then that when I saw it I did not immediately recognize it. I did not know which house it was.

It was not a house.

I looked up from the street below and walked on the sidewalk back and forth and then on the other side of the street. I looked up at (possible) window(s) of (possible) room(s) and couldn't remember which one. The earth didn't open beneath my feet. I didn't break down and cry.

There was a row, all slightly different but basically the same shade of white whether purplish or grayish or creamy colored. It was a sunny, lovely morning. Each was between another two or at an end, and each three stories tall, with nice big wide high sash windows, bright black shiny iron wrought gates, brass colored door knockers, ground floor doors below and first floor doors above, chimneys behind, and flower pots. I could not tell any one apart. (Actually one didn't have any flower pots. However, otherwise—)

I called it a house but it was not a house.

Maybe I'm wrong about other things. Maybe about a lot. What else I have called that wasn't that? What else have I forgotten? Is all that I remember wrong? Is everything not any more? Is this an end to this?